Emmy's DISCOVERY

Z. MINOR

Publishing Coordinator & Book Designer
Sharon Kizziah-Holmes

Paperback-Press
an imprint of Paperback Press, LLC
Springfield, Missouri

ISBN -13: 978-1-970560-25-1

Dedication

To my husband, John, your encouragement over the years makes my heart sing.

To my friends and writing ladies
Jana Dahmen
Kathy Pritchett
Linda Vick
Trisha Whitehill
Thank you for your encouragement and editing.
You all make me a better writer.

Thank you.

Prologue

Year – 1541, Rural England

Simon, the ringleader of the Gang of Six, stood watching with eagle eyes as five men moved up the tree-lined path. Once they passed him, he closed and locked the iron gate. This meeting was for members only. Flames blazed and danced from torches in every corner, bringing the dismal, stone-damp walls to life. Whispers of men talking bounced off the cavernous space. Water dripping down various rocks fed an underground stream. Fifty years ago, the cave became their secret meeting place.

The only element that changed over time was when a member died; a close relative, usually a son, would then take their place. Simon's grandfather had founded the 'Ruffians.' The townspeople called them 'The Badder Boys' because of their actions and attitudes.

Simon marched in and announced, "We have much to discuss. An opportunity has fallen into our laps, unbelievably, by the local townspeople that will give us more money than we can ever imagine."

He moved to stand in front of a small, carved wooden table. "I'm sure you have heard about our King's plan to remove the Catholic Church from England. He plans to create an English Church. One he can control more to his liking. His guards will loot all the riches they find in cathedrals, monasteries, nunneries, and priories for the King's war chest and personal use.

The local townspeople want to halt King Henry's greed by looting the items before his knights can reach them. The plan is to give us these priceless relics so we may hide them from the King's men before they strip the buildings bare."

One man stood. "What be in it for us?"

"We're taking these priceless treasures worth their weight in gold. We not be telling a living soul where we stash them. Once the King's men stop looking for the treasures, we'll sell them for more money than we can imagine. We'll only share the cash with the Ruffians. Believe me, the amount of money will be worth the wait.

"If we agree to this plan, we must find a secret location to store these valuables. All those in favor of this plan, stand."

There was no hesitation. All the men stood.

"Are there any questions? Think hard. After tonight, we'll not discuss this outside of our cave. The next meeting will be here in three days at midnight.

"Beginning tomorrow, each of you'll take an area of the countryside and search for a secret hideaway to keep our treasures hidden from the King's guards." He glanced around to make sure everyone was listening. "They'll question everyone as they search the countryside looking for the artifacts once they discover they are missing."

Each man took his verbal assignment from Simon, reached for a tankard, and filled it from the jugs on the table. Thus, ending the meeting.

In three months, they found the perfect hiding place. Each item would receive protection from moisture and remain safe. Once the members secured the goods in the hideout, each swore an oath not to approach the location or discuss the treasure.

Chapter 1

May 1822, Rural England

Since his mother's death two years ago, Greyson Hadden had continued living with his father and brother on the family estate. Life before her death had always been a trial. With his entire being, Greyson felt that his mother kept his father and brother on an even keel, at least most of the time.

Since her passing, his father and brother had become obsessed with ordering Greyson around. "Do this, do that." It never ended. His life got worse once Greyson's dearest grandfather died and left everything in his estate not entailed to him. When his father's and brother's gambling increased, so did their demands.

Their latest plan was to demand that Greyson marry the young chit next door. They needed her dowry to pay off their accumulated gambling debts. Over time, Greyson learned the best way to handle their demands was to ignore them, until now. He packed a small bag of his most cherished possessions after overhearing them planning a ball to announce his engagement. As he rode out of the estate gates, he wondered about the sudden change in his life and where he would go.

It didn't take long to remember the long-standing invitation to visit a family friend, Brishen, at the Roma camp.

An archaeology study had once again replaced Emmy Highbridge. It wasn't that she wasn't qualified or competent because she had proved many times that her abilities were sound. Emmy had more than met all of society's requirements.

No, being a mere woman had disqualified her. The London Archaeological Society didn't allow women as members. The men in charge told her. "You're welcome to take notes, make tea, and catalog items discovered by men, nothing more."

She returned to her older sister and brother-in-law's Woodhaven Estate in London to sulk and feel sorry for herself. Since childhood, her dream had been to become a world-famous archaeologist in her own right.

The house remained quiet as everyone was out enjoying the beautiful spring weather. The sun shone through the leaves on the trees and warmed even the city's darkest corners. Perfect weather brought many people to the parks. Emmy thought of walking in the park, but couldn't get enough energy to move.

The butler entered the library and announced. “Miss Emmy, Duke St. George is here and wishes to see you.”

“Are you sure he wants to see me?”

“Yes, Miss, he specifically asked for you.”

“Please show him to the sitting room and bring refreshments.”

Emmy quickly checked the hall mirror to make sure she looked presentable.

His request to see me has me puzzled. I haven’t spoken or seen him since Nicola and Clay’s wedding.

Emmy fidgeted, waiting for The Duke to appear. She grew increasingly nervous with every passing minute.

Once the butler shut the door, the Duke, in a most pleasant voice, stated, “Good afternoon, Emmy. I hope I’m not being forward in calling you by your first name or just showing up at the doorstep without an appointment.”

“Thank you, Sir. I’m honored. Won’t you please sit down?” She motioned to the chair near the fireplace as a chill swept through the room. “Refreshments will arrive soon. I didn’t realize you were in London. Nicola and Clay will be disappointed that they missed you.

“I didn’t come to London to see them. I came to meet with you regarding an opportunity I have and sincerely hope you will become part of my plan.”

The refreshments arrived. The butler poured a glass of brandy for the Duke and a cup of tea for Emmy before he left.

“I must admit, I’m intrigued. Currently, I’m at

my leisure and, of course, interested in any opportunity you might present."

"Let me start at the beginning. The Duchess and I recently purchased the old Rockhurst Estate. It has existed since before the Middle Ages. The manor house and the hunting lodge are in excellent condition. We completed extensive work on both buildings. They are now more than livable.

"Near the hunting lodge is a medieval village with two stone buildings. This period in England's history has always intrigued me. I would like to see if we can find historical information about our country during those intriguing times."

"Sir, I would love to take on a project such as this. It has always been a dream of mine. However, do you realize you'll receive many objections from the London Archaeology Society if you put a woman in charge of such a historically significant place? Believe me, I have great experience dealing with them."

"My dear, you come highly recommended by two of my favorite people, my son and daughter-in-law, and many of yours and my acquaintances. If you would like, you can reside in the hunting lodge, which has ample space for staff to ensure your safety and accommodate any additional personnel you may need to hire. Please say yes, or at least promise me you will consider my offer and give me an answer to my proposal within a week."

"Dearest Duke, I can give you my answer right now, depending on your answer to my following question. Who will manage this project?"

"You, my dear. I'll give you the authority to

manage the project as you see fit, and you can hire the necessary personnel. As a curious individual, I'll not question what you are doing, but I'll inquire about your progress. I've not set a deadline for completing the project because I do not know what you'll discover."

I can't believe this opportunity; I want to shout and twirl around the room. Smiling inwardly, I know I'll have to wait for him to leave.

"Then, Sir, I accept the position you have offered me. I would like a written agreement, so no one interferes with our working relationship."

"As you begin to make your plans. I'll return in a few days with a contract and the first installment of your wages. At that time, we'll discuss moving you to the hunting lodge if you have no objections."

"Thank you, Sir. Staying at the lodge will be the most convenient option. There are no words to express my appreciation for your faith in my abilities."

"Your acceptance of this undertaking pleases me; I know we'll achieve success together. I'm looking forward to seeing you next week."

Emmy escorted the Duke to the front door and wished him a pleasant afternoon. She locked the door, spun through the library, and collapsed into a chair.

Chapter 2

May 1822, Rural England

Within a week, the Duke supplied a comfortable carriage for her use. Emmy found she still had a minor worry that a man—or men—from the London Archaeology Society would try to take over her life-changing career opportunity.

Once she arrived at the Rockhurst Hunting Lodge, Emmy had difficulty believing she had arrived at this promising opportunity. It has been a whirlwind time getting everything ready to leave London. She gathered all her supplies, some of which she wasn't even sure she would need. Experience taught her the importance of being prepared, as she was uncertain about the supplies available in the nearest town to the Rockhurst Estate.

She refused to let anything cloud her positive

thinking. Emmy learned long ago that searching for problems was futile. Her suspicious thinking vanished, replaced by confidence as she strolled outside. Draping her wool shawl around her shoulders, Emmy plopped down on the porch's top step and enjoyed the breeze. The fresh air and the graceful movement of the tall grass beyond the trimmed ground danced back and forth. She found that the movement settled her nerves.

Emmy, delighted by the outdoors, thought of the papers and files left to inspect in the trophy room, which seemed to call to her.

Scattered documents were on the floor in the trophy room, while others overflowed in wooden boxes. Piles littered the tops of the tables and desks. Nothing had moved, not even an inch, since she had taken up residence. However, the time had come to quit just looking at the paperwork. It was time to catalog everything into its proper place. She learned long ago in her childhood that organization made everything in life more manageable.

Part of the reason she disliked going into the trophy room was that there wasn't an empty place in the room to hang a mirror, even a tiny one. Every wall displayed painted pictures of men standing next to the dead animals they had killed. The bedroom stairway walls also displayed pictures of dead animals. The sight upset her stomach whenever she walked into the trophy room or was on the stairs. If she looked at them too long, she gagged.

Emmy would hopefully come up with a solution. Earlier in the week, she hid animal pelts that had been used as rugs in the trophy room behind some boxes. She planned to keep them in their new home for as long as she lived at the lodge.

She sifted through old records from centuries past, stored in boxes Mr. Murphy, the butler, had brought into the sitting room. The Duke and Duchess of Saint George offered their massive library for her use. Over the centuries, the English language has developed, and any scholar must, at times, study ancient academic texts to understand their true meaning.

Mr. Murphy walked into the room with a tall man trailing behind him. "Excuse me, Miss. This gentleman has requested an audience with you."

The pleasant-looking man bowed in her direction after walking around the butler. "I'm Mr. Greyson Hadden. I'm a long-time friend of Brishen Draper. He requested I deliver the caravan outside to you and give you an important message."

Emmy was so captivated that she stood and stared at him. Mr. Murphy cleared his throat, causing her to blink several times.

"Oh, where are my manners? Please sit down," Emmy motioned to a chair in the sitting room. "May I offer you tea, sweets, or a midday meal?"

"I would appreciate a cup of tea. The roads were especially dusty today. However, I must take care of the horses and the caravan. Where do you wish me to stable them?"

Before Emmy could reply, Mr. Murphy stated, "Follow me, Sir. We'll get everyone settled in their new home."

Emmy watched the two men leave. She returned

to the trophy room and her paperwork, but didn't touch anything. Her thoughts were on Mr. Hadden.

Who is that man? I have never seen him at the Roma camp, nor have I ever heard his name mentioned. I know I would have remembered.

The housemaid scurried to the sitting room. "Mr. M., I be telling Miss Highbridge you be back. Cook made Cornish pasties. I placed them on the table along with the silverware and napkins."

The maid then hurried to the trophy room door. Just as she was ready to knock, Emmy opened the door.

The maid curtsied. "Mr. M., him put your guest in the sitting room."

"Thank you, Ivy. Who is Mr. M.?"

Ivy turned at the doorway. "That be Mr. Murphy." She left without a second glance at Emmy.

Emmy stood in the doorway, scrutinizing her guest. She noted his black, wavy hair curling around his ears, making him appear dashing and most appealing. He was tall compared to her tiny, five-foot-two-inch stature. Emmy decided this wasn't the time or place for daydreaming or wishful thinking.

"Good afternoon, Sir. Having been here for only two weeks, I've had no reason to venture to the stable. Are the accommodations for the horses and the caravan adequate?"

"Yes, they are more than acceptable. A trained horse accompanies each caravan. I expect the remaining caravan, the lads, and their cart to arrive in a week or two."

"Oh, I see. The cook sent you a midday meal. We may sit at the table, and once you finish your meal, we can discuss why you are here." Mr. Hadden ate and discussed his uneventful trip to Rockhurst. They moved to the chairs in front of the fireplace as the afternoon grew cooler.

"You mentioned Brishen sent you?"

"Yes, he requested I stay at Rockhurst and assist you in your archaeology excavation. Brishen has many contacts in England and beyond, and he is aware of the activities of many undesirable individuals. He recently discovered that many throughout England and beyond may have devious motives. They are seeking riches believed to exist in the old Rockhurst Village. Brishen has confirmed that some of these people have moved into the area. He requested I stay and assist you so no harm befalls you or those working with you."

"The only people I've engaged are three young lads from London who have become part of my extended family. I've no desire to employ extra workers for many reasons. First, they usually only come to steal. If the weather cooperates, I'll achieve my tasks within a reasonable time." Emmy sighed. "Now, I see the thieves are one step ahead of me. From my experience, I should have known it was only a matter of time."

"May I ask why you requested Roma caravans? It seems an old choice."

"When this archaeology opportunity presented itself, I realized some stable structures would be required. The inclement, changing English weather necessitates keeping many artifacts dry. Tents are flimsy structures that wind can quickly destroy, and thieves can efficiently enter, with no one wiser until it is too late. In previous endeavors, the thieves destroyed everything in their path. The caravans are lockable and easily moved from site to site, allowing me more control."

"Thank you for answering my questions. It makes perfect sense. I have a letter from Brishen for you. I'm sure it will explain his concerns." Mr. Hadden pulled an envelope from his jacket pocket and handed it to Emmy with a slight bow. "I would suggest you read it, and tomorrow morning at breakfast, we can discuss your concerns."

"Excellent idea. We eat our evening meal in a few hours. The entire house is usually up just as the sun is coming up, so bedtime is when the sun goes down or shortly after. You are welcome to stay in the small cottage near the stables. Mr. Murphy has assured me that one bedroom is ready for you."

Emmy rang the bell pull. Mr. Murphy came into the room within a second.

I sometimes suspect the butler eavesdrops at the door.

"Please show Mr. Hadden his room in the cottage."

"Yes, Miss. If you will follow me, Mr. Hadden. I'll escort you to your room and call on you for our evening meal."

"Thank you both. However, the excellent meal I just ate satisfied my hunger. Please thank the cook for me. I don't believe I would be worthy company this evening as I'm fatigued from my trip. Please wake me in time for breakfast, Mr. Murphy."

Emmy watched Mr. Hadden with great interest when the man strolled out the door. Turning to Mr. Muphy, she said, "Will you please have a horse saddled for me in the morning? No sidesaddle, please."

Continuing to pursue some of the material in the trophy room, Emmy was finally making sense of the paper stacks. The same family had owned the Rockhurst Estate for one hundred-plus years. The estate remained vacant for a long time after the death of the last family member. How and why the Duke and Duchess purchased the estate might prove interesting, as they appeared to own ample land in England and Scotland.

After her evening meal, as tired as she was, Emmy returned to the trophy room and made sense of more of the paperwork. When she felt her head nod forward more than once, Emmy finally realized it was time for bed. Taking the lantern, she banked the fire in the fireplace and plodded upstairs, yawning the entire way.

Once in bed, Emmy couldn't fall asleep. She tossed, turned, and wondered more than once who this mystery man, Mr. Hadden, was.

His manners and actions belong to a gentleman, not a gypsy. Mr. Hadden doesn't look like anyone from the camp. I visited Brishen most days and have gotten to know most of the Romas. I must not let him distract me from my task.

Falling asleep in the wee hours of the morning, Emmy dreamed of what she might find on the estate grounds, as it encompassed a sizeable area.

At precisely seven in the morning, Mr. Murphy entered the sitting room and announced Mr. Hadden's arrival for breakfast. After completing their morning English breakfast, they sat before the massive fireplace in the sitting room and enjoyed a second cup of tea. Emmy showed him the maps she had prepared for the day's outing.

Mr. Murphy knocked at the open door and entered. "The midday meals you requested are on a table at the back door. The horses are outside, as are the three special guests accompanying you."

"Who are our visitors?" Emmy frowned.

"It be best you see for yourself, Miss."

Noting the gleam in Mr. Murphy's eyes and the bounce in his step as he scooted out the door, Emmy smiled as he retreated through the door.

Shaking her head, she stated, "Well, Mr. Hadden, I think we should follow Mr. Murphy. Unless I miss my guess, he is up to something."

His actions don't surprise me because I believe he is a mischief-maker every chance he gets.

Chapter 3

Gathering their coats from the wooden chairs in the sitting room, they slipped them on as they walked to the back of the lodge. Emmy distinctly recognized Mr. Murphy's voice the closer she got to the door. The second voice she had never heard before. Rather than trying to guess who was waiting for them, once Mr. Hadden opened the door, Emmy strolled outside.

A cool, damp, penetrating wind greeted her as it whirled around. The sun poked through the clouds and then disappeared, only to reappear in typical English fashion. Dirt and leaves flew in different directions, changed course, and came barreling back toward them.

Two gigantic black dogs raced toward Emmy. They skidded to a stop mere inches from her, wagging their enormous tails. A young man towered over Mr. Murphy, who stood beside him.

The dog's huge, dark eyes studied her. Emmy

laughed as she reached out a hand toward them. They sniffed and moved their heads closer. Emmy took this as a sign she could pet them.

"What breed are these gigantic animals? They are dogs, aren't they?"

The young man stepped forward. "Excuse me, Miss. Let me introduce you to Jerkens and Petes. The one with the star on his forehead is Petes. He is older and thinks he is in charge. Duke St. George is the top breeder of English Mastiffs in all of Europe. Where these dogs go, so do I. My name is Joeson." He bowed his head to Emmy.

"It is a pleasure to meet you and your charges. I would like you to meet Mr. Hadden. I'm Miss Highbridge. As you can see, we are leaving to ride to the old village this morning. So, if you will excuse us."

"Oh, Miss, you don't understand. The dogs and I are here for your protection. I'm a former soldier, and where you go, so do the dogs and I."

"Is this necessary? I haven't requested guards." Emmy rubbed her hands together as they were becoming cold. She moved toward her horse, finally pulling gloves on from her pockets.

"That may be, Miss. However, I'll be coming with you. I've got my orders from His Grace. Reporting and seeing thieves roaming the woods has become a daily occurrence."

"Well, if you must come, then do so. I'll speak with His Grace later. However, please remember I'm in charge of the archaeology study at the old village. If you have questions, suggestions, or comments, please direct them to me."

The trio left at a canter, with the dogs running close behind. Emmy's riding attire made astride riding easy. She wore special trousers made by one of her older sisters, who owns a successful dress shop in London. Emmy wore a sturdy full-length wool dress. When she stood, the trousers under the dress vanished from view. Because Emmy wore custom boots, the cold and dampness that seemed to penetrate England never bothered her.

Her outer wool coat, made of two layers, came just below her hips, keeping her warm. She wore a fitted hat pulled down around her ears, which covered the rest of her hair, and a matching scarf graced her neck.

Both men wore heavy jackets, hats, and gloves. The old village wasn't far and soon came into view.

Mr. Hadden stopped and pointed to a cart in front of the first stone building. They all watched as two men emerged and threw something into the back of their cart. The men reentered the building. Taking a spyglass from his saddlebag, Mr. Hadden watched the men scurry out of the building again with something in their hands.

"It appears we have found some thieves at work." Emmy glanced at her companions. "We must proceed cautiously because I'm sure they have weapons."

"Joeson, take the dogs and go to the rear of the building." Mr. Hadden had not taken his eyes off the men. "Do you have a weapon?"

"Yes, Sir. A pistol, and I'm very proficient with my knife."

Using hand signals, Joeson and the dogs left

without making a sound. Emmy and Mr. Hadden advanced their horses toward the first building and the men's cart.

When the thieves saw them approaching, the men dropped the articles they were carrying and rushed back inside the building. Emmy and Mr. Hadden tied their horses to a portion of a falling-down fence, which, by all appearances, had once encircled the entire building.

Weeds and rubble concealed most of the building's lower exterior walls. The second stone building stood behind and to the side of the first one. Emmy hiked out to the cart. The wild grasses and weeds brushed against her knees.

Peering into the back of the wagon, she gathered up a stone slab. Once she turned it over, Emmy recognized the carving on the underside. It appeared to be from a game called Fox and Geese. The stone bench seat was likely from a cloister and was part of a carved or etched game board. Monks played this game during the Middle Ages. Mr. Hadden continued to observe the building, and the men marched out within a few minutes.

The larger of the two men glared at Mr. Hadden. "You best be off. You ain't welcome here and can't be stopping us." He stood with his legs apart, a large wooden club clenched in one hand.

His partner approached Mr. Hadden and pulled a pistol from his belt. "We be going to empty these here buildings."

"You realize you are on private property," stated Mr. Hadden. "These buildings belong to the Duke and Duchess Saint George and are part of the

Rockhurst Estate."

With a scowling face, the man with the gun stated. "Our boss, man, don't care who owns the land. 'im wants what 'im wants, which be everything in these here buildings. It be best you don't try to stop us."

The thieves ignored Emmy and didn't see her unfasten a whip from the hook on her belt and let the coil drop to the ground at her feet. She crept toward the men, who appeared to be observing Mr. Hadden.

When the man pointed his gun at Mr. Hadden again, Emmy dashed forward. She drew her arm back alongside her leg, then brought the whip before her as she snapped her wrist. Her whip shot forward.

The cracker's noise at the end of the whip caused both men to jump. The gun fell out of the man's hand—a three-inch red gash formed where the whip had struck him.

Emmy motioned with her hand—the agreed-upon signal to engage the dogs. Joeson sent the animals to watch over the two men, who were cowering on the ground. The dogs bared their teeth inches from the men's bodies.

"I would advise you not to move, or the dogs will tear you apart. It ain't a pretty sight," Joeson smirked as he walked over, tied the men's hands behind their backs, and marched them to the corner of the building. He made them sit down in the damp, cold dirt.

"You men best stay where I plant you." The dogs shadowed Joeson and moved to guard the men.

"Good dogs." He petted each dog and reached for their reward, a biscuit from his pocket. "Guard them well."

Emmy's curiosity propelled her to look inside the first building before Joeson could lock up the structures using the chains and padlock they had brought. The door would be secure and deter most thieves.

She remained in the doorway. The daylight allowed her to investigate the building. It appeared a windstorm had blown through the large room.

Furniture lay in pieces while a large dusty cloth covered some rubbish. A faint odor, likely a dead animal, lingered in the air.

In a word, it was a jumbled mess of this and that. Emmy found it hard to identify anything. They secured the door as best they could.

After some discussion, Joeson drove the cart with the men secured in the back. The dogs trailed behind, keeping a watchful eye on the thieves.

Mr. Hadden took Joeson's horse and led it back to the Lodge, with Emmy close behind. She placed the whip near her hand so that the men could see it.

What His Grace will say about these recent developments, I hope and pray, this won't change any plans for the archaeology study.

Chapter 4

Both thieves stuttered and stammered as they marched to the empty garden shed behind the lodge.

"Try to escape, and the dogs will track you down." Joeson grinned as he shut and locked the door. Mr. Murphy, Mr. Hadden, Petes, and Jerkens stood guard outside the building. Joeson rode to the manor house to inform the Duke of the men's apprehension.

Emmy's fingers itched to see what was in the cart. However, she gasped when she noticed the pitiful donkey. His ribs protruded. He hung his head, almost touching the ground, and he appeared as if he might collapse at any moment.

She needed help to move the horse and cart into the barn. Mr. Murphy predicted a cold, wet evening, suggesting a blanket for the horse and donkey. The stable lad promised to groom the donkey once the animal had eaten.

Emmy went to the cart and unloaded it. Her

anger grew as she realized everything was just a huge pile. They hadn't tried to protect any of the artifacts. She'd removed a small portion of the load when his Grace appeared.

"Morning, Miss Highbridge."

"Your Grace," she curtsied, "I hope we didn't interrupt your morning?"

"Not to worry yourself. I planned to ride over later to see how you progressed. I see you jumped right into the middle of the fray." The Duke shook his head as he walked over to look inside the wagon.

"Yes, we caught them stealing from one of the buildings. I'm sorry to say the men were reckless with everything they found. So far, I have made two piles of artifacts. One is a jumble of broken pottery pieces and other items; some appear to be in better condition, as they were on the top layers."

"I've sent Joeson to Reed, the largest town in the immediate area, where the sheriff has an office, which includes a jail. He informed me that the men said they worked for Samuel Potts, the pub owner in Reed.

"When we first purchased Rockhurst, I discovered Potts owns most of Reed and bullies everyone in town. Most people hate him for his underhanded dealings. This affair might prove more than interesting and, I must say, dangerous. I understand if you would like to rethink working on this project."

Mr. Hadden observed the estate entrance as the Duke and Emmy finished unloading the cart.

Two hours later, Mr. Hadden informed them that

two men and Joeson had just entered the property. Emmy rushed to the lodge's front yard after she covered the cart.

Dismounting, the men stood in a line. Joeson moved toward the horses as he gathered all the reins and moved them to a hitching rail out of everyone's way.

The man in the center moved forward. "Good afternoon, Your Grace." He bowed his head. "I've not had the pleasure of meeting you. My name is Richard Hide. I'm the sheriff. Welcome."

Standing next to the sheriff, a man moved forward. "I'm Samuel Potts, the proprietor of the Black Feather Pub in Reed. There appears to be a problem involving two of my hired men. I came to take charge of what I'm sure is a little misunderstanding."

Emmy, not one to hold back, stated. "It's much more than a bit of a misunderstanding. Your men were stealing from one of the old buildings on the Duke's property. Mr. Hadden, Joeson, and I caught them." By this time, Emmy had moved a few feet closer to the men.

"I don't believe this concerns you, Miss." Mr. Potts smirked at her. "This is between us, gentlemen."

Crossing her arms, Emmy took a deep breath and said, "Sir, you couldn't be more wrong in your assumption."

"I would like to know where my men are. You are holding them?"

Moving closer to Potts, Emmy announced, "Yes, we are. I plan to make a formal complaint against them." Mr. Hadden moved to stand beside Emmy.

"Miss, I've told you this is a matter for men, not a slip of a girl." Potts slapped the side of his leg with his gloves, which he had removed earlier.

The Duke nodded in Potts' direction as he cleared his throat. "Allow me to explain. I'm sure you will find this information fascinating and beneficial. Miss Highbridge is a trained archaeologist and very accomplished. Rockhurst's buildings on this property are why she is in residence.

"You'll be dealing with her concerning this incident and any others. Believe me when I say you don't want to deal with me. Do I make myself clear?"

"Well, well, I see the lay of the land." Potts scowled, his face turning red. "I wish to see my men."

Moving a little closer to Potts, Emmy announced. "All in due time, I want your word as a gentleman that the men you employ will cease entering the Rockhurst Estate."

Mr. Potts glared at her while she continued to look directly at him. "I demand to see my men."

"Sir, being a tyrant will not work to your advantage. You'll not get what you want. Ask politely, and I'll entertain your request."

"Sheriff, I demand you do something," Potts shouted.

"Miss Highbridge, may I see the men you are accusing of stealing?"

"Of course, please follow me." When Mr. Potts moved forward, Emmy stopped in mid-stride. "You,

Sir, will not accompany us."

At that moment, Jerkens and Petes came into view, emitting a low growl as they followed Emmy. Potts stopped in his tracks.

"Carry on, Miss Highbridge." His Grace motioned to the shed. "I'll wait here with Mr. Potts."

Mr. Hadden took Emmy's arm while the sheriff stepped behind them. The couple stood aside after unlocking the door. Both thieves fell out of the entryway into a muddy puddle.

"About time you get here." One man said, pointing to Emmy and Mr. Hadden. "These here people have been mistreating us. They have…"

Cradling his injured arm in a covered rag spattered with blood, the second man grimaced, stood, and stumbled forward.

Snickering, the sheriff asked, "What happened to you? Looks like your hand got caught where it wasn't supposed to be."

"Well, Potts, 'im wants what be in them buildings. There might be something valuable in them. He sent us to clean them out."

"You know, you and Potts or any of his men can't be on this property."

"So, Potts says we can."

"I don't care what Potts says. If you come here again, I'll take you to the authorities in London. So, take heed and stay clear of this place."

The loudmouth said, "Ain't never going to happen."

The sheriff motioned the men to walk to where their boss and the duke stood.

"I have informed your men that I'll take them to the authorities in London if they come on this property again, which includes any of your men. This property is off-limits to you. Are there any questions?"

Potts pointed to the injured man. "What is wrong with him? He didn't have any injuries when he left town this morning."

Before the man could gather his wits to answer the question, Emmy spoke up. "I'll be happy to inform you. Your man pointed a pistol at Mr. Hadden and said he would shoot him."

"I gots this nasty cut on me hand when her used a whip to take my gun away from me."

Hanging his head, the man kept his eyes looking at the ground.

"Are you telling me a mere girl disarmed you? What is this world coming to when a woman forgets where she belongs?"

Emmy said, "You remember, Mr. Potts, I protect what is mine. I'm responsible for this endeavor. I'll do what is necessary to keep thieves out of it and do what it takes to keep us safe."

Potts spat back, "What about my cart and donkey? They does belong to me."

"They do," Emmy said. "You'll get your property back. Once the cart is empty, and the poor, hungry donkey recovers from being mistreated."

Turning away from the men, Emmy and Mr. Hadden hurried back to the stable to finish unpacking the cart. They could hear Potts continue arguing with the sheriff. The thieves grumbled about the long walk back to town. Ultimately, their capture wasn't their fault. Next time, the loudmouth stated they would need more men.

Strolling up to Emmy, His Grace said, "I'll be at the lodge at nine in the morning to discuss what has taken place this day. I don't believe Mr. Potts will surrender his plan. Always, and I mean always, take the dogs with you, Miss Highbridge. We'll need a plan of action to protect us from this man and his ruthless gang. Never underestimate them."

Chapter 5

Early the next morning, the curtains filtered the bright light when the sun poked through the clouds, giving the room a warm glow. Emmy hurried downstairs to make sure the men were getting ready to leave for the village.

After eating, they gathered their jackets and headed outdoors—Emmy's excitement about exploring the buildings was contagious. Just the thought of what they would find had her almost dancing out the door.

Until Joeson announced, "Miss Highbridge, your dog training must occur before we proceed with any other activities. Only then will they listen to your commands."

"Is that necessary?" From the corner of her eye, Emmy watched the dogs wagging their tails and their tongues hanging out of their enormous mouths. She shook her head. "I can't imagine them paying attention to me."

"I recommend we work at the lodge for just a short time this morning. This way, new surroundings will not distract the dogs in the old village as they are learning to follow you and listen to your commands.

"You need to master only four commands. They already know them. However, they must recognize your voice, listen to only you, and follow your commands. It's for your protection."

"Well, if I must, I must. But first, I need to inform Mr. Hadden that you and I will be with the dogs for a short time. Please tell me this won't take all day."

"It will only take an hour at the most."

Emmy hurried to the back door and explained what she and Joeson would be doing. Greyson said he would enjoy another cup of tea.

She followed fast-moving Joeson as he went behind the barn to practice without being disturbed or distracted.

Joeson turned and faced Emmy once they were out of sight. "The commands are simple: come, stay, defend, and attack. If you hear the dogs growling, stop what you are doing and tell them to defend. They'll come to your side and protect you from harm.

"You must project your voice to overcome any noise or distractions. Starting today, you'll command the dogs. In that way, they'll understand they must obey you. These dogs are brilliant; in no time, they'll become your shadow."

Learning the directions took just a few minutes. Only twice did Joeson have to remind her to talk louder.

I received constant instructions to use proper speech and to speak softly, as it was most ladylike. She laughed out loud as she walked back to the lodge.

The trip to the buildings wasn't much later than planned.

Emmy gathered everyone together, as they still had plenty of time to work in the buildings.

Storage hadn't been high on my list because we had found nothing significant. I should make a plan for the collection as we progress. It's incredible how opportunities, or lack thereof, cause change when you least expect it.

"The more I think about it, someone has been stealing from at least the first building for a long time and dumping rubbish inside, which doesn't make much sense. Starting this search will be just the first of many."

"What is the most memorable item you have ever discovered?" Mr. Hadden asked Emmy, "I would think one would never know what one will find. This is the reason I've become so intrigued by archaeology."

Emmy laughed. "A few years ago, I found a beautiful ring — solid gold with a ruby the size of my thumbnail in dried-up cow dung."

"You aren't making this up, are you?"

"No, I was working on a site with young students. We were walking across a field, and most of them ambled around some dried dung, but not me. I wasn't paying attention to where I was walking and tripped when I took my next step. The dung pile split into two pieces. Stumbling, I glanced back, and the ring's gold edge poked through the pile's center."

"The property owner presented me with the ring and thanked me for all my hard work with the students."

"How did it find its way into a pile of dung, do you think? Do you still have the ring?"

"I do not know how the ring got to where it was or its age. To be honest, archaeology is fascinating. One never knows where something will appear, or why. When we return to London, I'll gladly show you my prize."

Shortly after lunch, Emmy announced it was time to return to the lodge. She had paperwork to do and unload the cart.

Later, Joeson strolled up to the couple just as they closed the barn door. "Mr. Hadden, would you like to come to Reed with me this evening? I need to check on my parents' well-being. My father had a serious run-in with Potts, and he continues to harass them almost daily or whenever he sees them in town."

"I would like to see what this town looks like, and I will happily accompany you. I can't imagine Potts likes you working at Rockhurst."

"The two of you might gather information about what he is up to." Emmy yawned.

"Old man Potts offers me a job every time I see him. He has threatened me a time or two as well. I'm always on guard in town and stay off Main Street when possible."

"Be extra careful. I'll inform Mr. Murphy you

won't be here for the evening meal," Emmy said. "Remember the potential danger in Reed."

The men departed. Emmy was looking forward to a quiet afternoon when voices from the porch echoed. She stood and waited for Mr. Murphy to inform her who was calling.

Chapter 6

"Miss, per The Duke's instructions, the men are here to move the furniture out of the upstairs rooms and replace it with tables as you requested. You can provide information about removing the hunter portraits and animal heads from the trophy room and the stairway.

"Thank you, Mr. Murphy. I'll follow you as I look forward to the pictures and the animal heads being gone."

Emmy couldn't believe how fast they worked until Mr. Murphy told her the man in charge had recruited four workers from the farm to help them. The men had removed everything by the end of the day. Three bedrooms, which the lads would use, were ready for their arrival.

After the evening meal in the trophy room, Emmy heard someone knocking on the back door. Within a few seconds, Mr. Murphy stood in the doorway. "Miss, two men want to see you. His

Grace requested that they come to introduce themselves. Shall I show them in, or do you want to go to the door?"

Carrying her pistol in her dress pocket gave Emmy a sense of safety when meeting strangers. She usually had it wherever she went. Emmy stood next to the chair in the sitting room. Its proximity to the fireplace radiated warmth.

Two men, their hats in their hands, followed Mr. Murphy into the room. The man with white hair was older and obviously in charge.

"Miss Highbridge, His Grace, requested that my son and I guard the grounds around the lodge and the barn. My name is James, and my son's name is Keller."

Keller bowed his head toward Emmy.

"It's a pleasure to meet you both. The duke mentioned you would be coming by to introduce yourself. I appreciate your efforts to keep us safe."

James moved forward. "Do you have any questions, Miss?"

"No, not presently. Mr. Hadden and Joeson have gone to Reed. I'm unsure how long they will be there. Both men are staying in the guesthouse to the left of the Lodge."

"We met them just as they were leaving. We'll take care to watch for their return."

"Thank you. Petes and Jerkins are in the barn guarding the items we recovered from one of the village buildings."

"We are familiar with both dogs; believe me, we'll stay clear of them."

"I can bring them into the lodge until the men

return, if you like?"

"No, there is no need for you to do so. Thank you for your offer."

"The duke told me you are sleeping in a temporary hut. I'm asking because we have an additional caravan, which, when it arrives, I would be pleased to offer to you for your use."

"Thank you, but I don't think one with flowers and such on the side will keep us hidden from the thieves."

Emmy laughs. "You haven't seen the one painted green. I'll let you know when it arrives. You can review it and decide whether it meets your needs. You won't have to pay to use it."

"We will come by as soon as the caravan arrives. Thank you for your kind offer."

"I know I'll sleep better knowing you both are protecting the lodge."

After the men departed, Emmy noticed Mr. Murphy standing by the open door. "If you don't mind my saying, Miss, you are right smart." He turned and quickly left.

I wonder what he meant. Mr. Murphy continues to surprise and amaze me at every turn.

Emmy rubbed her neck and was pleased to find that all hunting portraits and trophies were gone from the trophy room. Walking up the steps to her bedroom, she felt an added relief that she didn't have to look at dead animal pictures.

Pulling back the bedcovers, she stopped and sat on the edge of the bed.

I promised myself I would not dream of Mr. Hadden. After all, I'm sure he is way out of my reach. He's likely here because of the lack of a better alternative. He acts like a titled man, yet something is missing. His clothes are of the finest quality, yet he presents himself as ordinary. I wonder. I guess time will tell.

Emmy got into bed and fell asleep.

The next morning, she was ready to face the new day and any problems that came her way. Emmy sat, enjoying her second cup of tea, when Mr. Murphy announced Joeson and Mr. Hadden.

"They are most hopeful they could have breakfast with you," announced Mr. Murphy with a broad smile as the two men entered the room.

"Please request the cook to prepare breakfast for them and make a standing directive with the kitchen staff. The two men will have breakfast here daily and, most often, their evening meal as well. I'll explain their meal situation directly to the men."

"Very well, Miss."

The men strolled into the room, and Emmy motioned them to the table. "I hope we haven't inconvenienced either of you?" Removing his jacket, Mr. Hadden placed it on the back of his chair. "After a dreadful time trying to make something edible this morning, we have decided that neither of us can cook."

"Please do not worry. I have just informed Mr. Murphy to have the kitchen staff prepare breakfast for both of you and any other meals as required. Please speak with him if you need to make any changes to this arrangement."

"Thank you. I hate cooking, which I've been trying to do in the kitchen in our quarters with little success." Joeson frowned and looked down at the tabletop.

"This eating arrangement will allow us to make our daily plans and allow both of you to accommodate my schedule. I realize and expect you both, from time to time, to have personal business arise."

"I don't know about Joeson, but I'm starving. We didn't eat last night. I was too busy amassing information. Let me tell you, Potts is a tyrant."

"Why am I not surprised?" Emmy shook her head.

The men sat, devoured their meal, and left nothing on their plates. They had just finished refilling their coffee when they heard His Grace talking to Mr. Murphy as they walked into the room.

"Good morning. We have much to discuss. I'm not sure where to start. Miss Highbridge, would you begin with your approach to our project?"

"First, I would like to move into the sitting room, which is more comfortable, Mr. Murphy. Please bring fresh tea and coffee."

They were sitting in chairs around a small wooden table in no time. Earlier, Emmy arranged a map in the center, offering a clear view of the estate.

CHAPTER 7

"Please stop me if anything I say is not clear. We need to make it difficult, if not impossible, for anyone to determine where we plan to store the artifacts. Putting them in any of the outbuildings will allow thieves to break in and steal whatever they wish.

"Mr. Murphy and I walked through the entire lodge early this morning. The cellar would be the ideal place for storing items that are not affected by a dirt floor or dampness. We moved the furniture from three of the upstairs bedrooms and replaced the furnishings with tables and cupboards to store the more delicate items."

"Thank you, Sir, for having your men remove everything, including the hunting pictures."

"My pleasure, I disliked the pictures as much as you do," replied the Duke.

"One bedroom will become a workroom for cleaning and repairing any articles discovered. The first thing that comes to my mind is the pottery pieces. The attic can take any overflow, depending on the number of items. We'll work most days at the site if the weather is good. Once we gather items, we'll have plenty of work to keep us busy, especially if the weather turns unpleasant."

"I judge this to be a workable arrangement," The Duke said. "I hate to mention the following. Unless you are in the lodge, you must always have someone working with you. Locking the door during this trying time is most necessary."

"When the Duchess and I first moved here, I had Mr. Potts investigated. Information continues to come to me. Yesterday, I received some disturbing details from London. He is very deceitful, and he hired thugs who are just as bad. The two you met yesterday are most likely the best of the bunch. The rest are rugged, uncouth, cruel men. They'll go to great lengths to accomplish Potts' directives. So, make no mistakes. They are evil, the entire lot of them."

"You met two of my hired guards last night, whom I trust and who I have every confidence in. They won't betray us. Do you know when the lads will be here? Will they be able to handle what might be on the horizon?"

"Speaking of your hired guards, they'll come to look at the second caravan when it arrives. I offered it to them to use as their quarters, which would be much safer than their hut."

"My helpers should be here soon. I received a letter yesterday informing me that the lads should arrive in less than a week. Mr. Hadden, you agreed to the arrival time when we met."

"Yes, you are right. I could travel to the camp and find out the schedule, but I hate leaving with everything so unsettled."

"Do you think I could go?" Joeson stood and moved to stand in front of the fireplace. "Would anyone from the Roma Camp give me any information?"

"I know without a doubt. The Roma won't give you any information and most likely won't even talk to you. You would get the silent treatment." Shrugging his shoulders, Mr. Hadden raised his eyebrows.

Emmy hesitated and said, "Yesterday's purpose was exploring, but plans frequently change, and they will continue changing. Today, I want all of us to see the buildings and explore their interiors. We must lock everything up. We will not be storing items in the barn or any other buildings."

His Grace stood. "You appear to be handling everything. People talk; some Rockhurst workers and servants live in or around Reed. So, anything they hear or see might end up in Potts's hands. Just keep me apprised of your progress. Be careful. That evil man will not give up. I've met his kind many times, and disaster always follows them.

"I'll return tomorrow morning. Please remember I've no intention of interfering with your goals and plans. As I mentioned, I'm very curious. By the way, I can and will hire more guards if necessary. Any questions?"

Emmy heard voices outside as His Grace was ready to walk out the front door. Her face broke into a huge smile. "I believe the lads have arrived." Laughing, she hurried to the front door. "Now the fun and mayhem will begin."

Abruptly, Mr. Murphy entered. He'd moved in front of her.

"I'll be opening the door, Miss."

"Yes, Mr. Murphy." She drew back and suppressed a smirk. She couldn't wait to see the others' reaction to the young lads. His Grace, Mr. Hadden, and Joeson moved next to Emmy.

Eel, being the leader of this threesome, moved forward. "We be helpers to Miss Highbridge, Miss Emmy." He grinned and bowed his head. "I be called Eel." He pointed to his mates. "He be Jimmy and him be Jeb."

Emmy whispered, more to herself than anyone else. Eel has gathered some new manners since I last saw him. I wonder how long it will last. She smiled.

The lads wore new clothes — dark trousers, shoes, and jackets — to keep them warm. I hoped they had brought work clothes with them. If not, I will take them to town to purchase some sturdy work clothes.

Eel noticed Emmy. He poked Jimmy in the ribs, and Jimmy poked Jeb. They all danced around Mr. Murphy and ran to hug Emmy. Mr. Murphy harrumphed and then chuckled.

"I'm so happy to see all of you. I believe introductions are in order." She walked over and stood in front of the duke. "I would like you all to meet Duke St. George. We'll be working on his property, which is called Rockhurst."

Each boy bowed his head, and Eel said, "It be a pleasure and honor to meet you, Your Grace."

Emmy then introduced Mr. Hadden, Joeson, and Mr. Murphy. The boys' ages ranged from ten to almost twelve, with Eel the oldest, making him the leader. They shook hands with everyone but the duke, who left within a few minutes.

The rest lingered in the foyer until the outside door closed. Emmy led everyone to the sitting room.

"We need to sit at the table and talk without shouting across the room. You, lads, didn't have any difficulty finding Rockhurst, did you?"

Before the boys could answer, Mr. Hadden said, "I assumed Brishen would have some of his people travel with you."

"Him did. They turned back when we come to the place on the road with an arrow pointing to Reed. Then we followed the road sign to Rockhurst. Mr. Brishen taught us how to shoot a pistol and gave each of us one. Them be in our wagon. No one bothered us. Me thinks the Roma wagon, and the Gypsies scared them away." The boys beamed from ear to ear.

"Have you eaten this day? Emmy touched Jeb's arm as she sat next to him.

"No, and sure, be hungry."

Mr. Murphy said, "Upon their arrival, I requested the cook make them a proper English breakfast. We couldn't let the lads starve after their long trip. Where should they be served, Miss?"

"If it is no problem to serve their breakfast in here. We have plans to make for the day."

Small talk and laughter ran around the table regarding the lads' trip. They had taken turns driving the Roma Caravan and their cart. The lads enjoyed the journey as they had never left London before.

Chapter 8

Emmy, in truth, was glad they came and got away from the problems of the gangs in London, who, by all reports, appeared to be getting out of control. The London streets were perilous at night and were no longer safe. During the daytime, some parts of London also became unsafe.

The government arrested any groups of young men who appeared to be in a gang and transported them to Australia and the colonies.

Listening to the lads delighted Emmy as they gave her news of her dear family. She hadn't realized she missed the lads and enjoyed their antics. It gave her time to remember when they had come into her family's life.

I wonder if I'm getting along with Mr. Murphy. I've been doing for myself that there are times I find it difficult for him to catch up to my quick thinking, most of the time. After all, I'm operating in a man's environment, and he might sometimes find it hard to understand my woman's reasoning.

The food arriving stopped Emmy's thinking and the chatter of the lad's discussion of the trip. The boys ate as if they hadn't eaten in a week. While they finished their meal, Emmy explained their previous day and their current plans for the day. She recognized the signs as the boys squirmed in their chairs, eager smiles spreading across their faces as they lived for any hunt.

Emmy was determined to pay the lads for the use of their cart and their work. It would give them some money to spend and make them paid workers.

Everyone was eager to leave for the village until the Duke suddenly returned with four men whom they had never seen.

"I'll not be staying long. My land agent has requested a meeting, but I felt you needed to meet the four men I had come from a different estate to ensure your safety.

Emmy observed a man lagging, his head averted, his face concealed. Jimmy walked toward the man.

Eel thrust his arm out in front of his friend. "Leave him be. I be explaining later."

Like his mates, Eel stood next to Mr. Hadden. Once the Duke and the men had left, Emmy looked at the boys. "I noticed you lads started acting strange when His Grace reappeared."

"We knows one of the men. He be called Willie." Eel shook his head.

"I'm surprised he didn't come and talk to you?" Emmy chewed on her lip.

"I think he be hiding or trying to. Him didn't want us to recognize him," Jeb said.

"We've done some dealings with him in London. He wanted our help in shady dealings just before him suddenly left town." Eel rocked back and forth on his heels. "We told him no, then he disappeared. I figured he be in trouble with the Bow Street Runners. Not be sure."

"I'll mention your comments to His Grace," Joeson said, wrinkling his brow.

Mr. Hadden helped Emmy down from her horse once they reached the village site. "Miss Highbridge, where do you want to start?"

"Before we begin, I would like to name the buildings so everyone will know which one to go to when we talk about them. I'm considering holding a contest!"

"Someone hollered out, "Splendid idea."

If I stand still, close my eyes, and ignore the noise, I can almost picture the village alive. There would have been a blacksmith shop, a gathering place that most likely served spirits of some type, possibly a bakery, and other stores, depending on the population. I can almost determine when the buildings stood. They most likely were wooden structures with thatched roofs, which is why they disappeared hundreds of years ago.

Eel touched her arm, which brought her back to the present. "Miss Emmy, we are ready for the contest."

Everyone started shouting out names all at once. Some were silly, while others were too long and confusing.

"Stop. You can't all shout out names at the same time. I must write them down so we can vote;

whichever name has the most votes will win."

Emmy talked to each person, collected their names, and wrote them in her book. Once she had written the names down, they voted for the winners. Stone Cottage's name was the first building. The Farmhouse became the name of the second building. Jeb beamed because he had submitted both names.

Emmy, Mr. Hadden, and Joeson left on horseback.

The boys rode in their cart, a reward from the London Bow Street Runners for helping solve a significant crime. Their wagon had allowed the lads to earn money in London by moving items for people and to gain some independence. The Earl of Woodhaven, Emmy's brother-in-law, paid the upkeep on the cart, stabled the horse, and occasionally used their services.

The enormous dogs fascinated the lads. Every time they came close enough, the boys would pet them, which Petes and Jenkins enjoyed. Of course, the treats offered to their new furry friends brought the dogs back whenever they had the chance.

I sure enjoy watching the dogs and the lads. They are all looking for adventure or mischief, depending on how I view it. I can't help but smile when I observe their antics.

As the Stone Cottage was the closest building to the road and had been the one the thieves had broken into, they decided to start there.

Emmy asked everyone to gather around her so she could lay out her plan. "I must know where the artifact comes from. Everyone must realize that moving an item makes it impossible to return to its original place. Someone in the near or distant future may need to know the origin of an item for historical reasons. Therefore, it's essential to know the original location. Even if we consider it might end up in the throwaway pile."

"Jeb, go pick up something from the dirt path." Emmy pointed to an area.

"Why do we gots to do that?" Jeb's vacant look made his comment very clear to the adults.

He did and brought a small rock to her. Opening her book, she wrote Stone Cottage in large letters on the first line.

"The person reading our ledger in the future might have to know where the rock came from, or at least the general area."

On the first line, she wrote the date. On the following line, she wrote the number one, then noted a description that read: small dirt rock—color unknown due to caked dirt covering it. She made sure the entire group saw and read her entry.

"Eel, Jimmy, and Jeb, I want you all to walk back and forth in the area where Jeb picked up the rock. Then, one of you take a rake from the cart and push the dirt back and forth."

Laughter echoed as the boys made a general mess of the area.

"Jeb, I want you to return the rock to where you found it."

"I gots no idea where that there spot would be, cause we messed it all up. We did."

"Correct. Moving an item usually prevents it from returning to the same spot. Each article needs a proper listing for future reference, like the dirt rock found 3 feet from the willow tree's base and 10 feet from the footpath's start. We'll record detailed location data for each article.

"Another example would be a book. '*The Road Beyond*'. Its location was two feet from the doorway of the Stone Cottage. I'll be the keeper of this list. For everything you find, you must come to Mr. Hadden or me so that one of us can list the items in the book. There are no exceptions. We will record all found items in this book.

"Each of you will look for artifacts in your assigned areas. It'll be up to each of you to bring your items to me or Mr. Hadden and identify them.

"I'll assign who is working in which building in a few minutes. Each of you will look for artifacts in your designated areas."

Chapter 9

"There is a space in the building to store some items when we get more organized. We'll also have an outside facility designated as a disposal area. Either Mr. Hadden or I will tell you if you should put something there. Cleaning both buildings will take some time. When I took a quick peek into the building, I saw a lot of garbage.

"Tonight and every night, we'll put all the items in the cart and take them to the lodge. There are tarps under the cart seat to cover the items, so if anyone shows up uninvited, they cannot see what we have found. We must also make a temporary fence to keep animals and unwanted people away from the trash pile. We'll bring the caravan to the site tomorrow to house any saved items. Any questions?

"Let's clear out the unwanted items at Stone Cottage together. It's a mystery why someone didn't dispose of them outdoors or give them away.

If you are tired of working in your building, contact Mr. Hadden or me. We'll find other work for you lads to do."

They paused for tea from the crockery pot, which had kept the beverage warm, and some berry scones the cook had just baked. Even the dogs received treats from Mr. Murphy.

They labored all day, pausing for small breaks as the work became tedious. Jeb found two belt buckles, which appeared crusted with dirt and grime. Emmy planned to clean them in the evening to see if she could date them. Occasionally, one of the other lads would arrive with an item for Emmy to examine and record in her book. At this point, their findings had suffered significant damage, or parts were missing.

Someone is watching me. The hair on the back of my neck is tingling. I must walk about to see if I notice anyone in the distance.

Emmy strolled around the perimeter of the building. Petes and Jerkens followed her. She threw sticks for them to fetch. Petes was the fastest of the two, so she started throwing two sticks simultaneously.

She laughed at their antics and glanced around as they played their game, hoping to glimpse movement in the trees. Emmy saw two deer watching her and the dogs.

Joeson told me that ten puppies were born just a few days ago. I might ask His Grace if I could purchase one. A dog might give me peace of mind, knowing it would protect me once it grew up and keep me company. I will have to think about this.

Emmy hurried back to the Stone Cottage. They started packing up for the day just as it began to mist. For safekeeping, Mr. Hadden deposited some bundles of wrapped artifacts from the Farmhouse.

Mr. Hadden cleared his throat to get Emmy's attention. "Burning all the discarded items tomorrow when we return would be best. Otherwise, the pile will become unmanageable."

"That's an excellent suggestion. But we must find some material to cover the pile to protect it from the rain, or we won't be able to burn it. You could teach the lads how to manage a fire if you have no problem with them doing so." Suddenly, an enormous boom sounded nearby, followed by a flash of lightning. "We'd best leave, as it sounds like a storm is getting closer."

The lads and Mr. Hadden located some large wooden boards and covered the pile.

Mr. Hadden helped Emmy to mount her horse. The rain started as they left the village. The rain deluged them as they arrived at the lodge. Everything found a place in record time.

They groomed and fed the horses. After changing their wet clothes, they found delicious tea and sweet cakes waiting for them on the sideboard.

Once Emmy got everyone's attention, she announced, "I trust we will find artifacts that align with what we are seeking once we pass the top level. The flower caravan will become our storage unit. Our work will continue tomorrow, just as it did today. The lads will be in charge of storing all our tools and repairing them as needed.

"Doing this will save us time transporting them

every day and allow us to escape the rain and cold if necessary. If need be, we can even change clothes.

"Mr. Hadden will secure sufficient indoor workspace in each building, thereby eliminating the weather's impact on our work. Let's hope the weather cooperates with our schedule. Be sure to bring some extra clothing tomorrow if the rain continues. Can we get enough wood to build an enclosure for the horses to keep them out of any inclement weather?"

"I believe there is still ample wood in the barn," Mr. Hadden commented. "Later this evening, the lads and I'll explore the area and load up what is there, allowing us to get an early start." He walked over to where the table sat against the wall. "I want to look at the map a little closer. I think I saw the remnants of another building near our site when I took a stroll this afternoon."

Emmy joined him as he inspected the pile of maps she had placed in the sitting room earlier that morning.

He picked up a chart. "I believe this is the one I wanted."

"Wonderful. I'm going to peruse some of the old journals. I might have overlooked some information about other buildings." Emmy plopped down in a chair near the table.

I'm still curious about you, Mr. Hadden. I know Brishen sent him, but there must be more to the story. He is remarkably kind to the lads and me. Yet, I sense he is more than he pretends to be. Besides, I'm uncertain why Brishen sent him. Yes, to deliver the caravan, but to remain here to help me. Hmm, I wonder? I find him fascinating, and Mr. Hadden seemed interested in archaeology. Or can it just be my wishful dreaming?

Joeson left to tend to the dogs. Eel and his mates were right behind him. The room plunged into silence. Emmy walked into the trophy room, and the trophies and pictures were all gone. Further examination of the room revealed that her hidden rugs had disappeared. Hadden walked into the room.

"Mr. Hadden, might I ask you a question?"

"Of course, ask away."

"I don't understand why Brishen asked you to stay. He never mentioned you in any of our conversations, not once. I also never saw you at the Roma camp. Before I went to London, I had spent most days at the Roma Camp or at my foster parents' home. "

Mr. Hadden sighed. "Well, I was seeking a place to get away from my family. It is rather a long story and…"

Mr. Murphy entered the room and announced that the evening meal was ready. Much to Emmy's disappointment, the butler waited and escorted them into the sitting room.

The smell of food made Emmy's mouth water. She hoped to carry on their conversation when a loud clatter of noise announced the lads, with Joeson trailing behind them.

"How did you know the evening meal was on the table?" Emmy asked the room at large.

"Oh, Miss, there be a bell outside the back door. Mr. Murphy uses it to ring for meals."

"How clever…I must be sure and thank him. He is watching out for all of us."

Emmy invited everyone into the trophy room after they enjoyed their excellent meal of lamb, potatoes, fresh salad, and many vegetable dishes. They enjoyed plentiful servings of plum pudding and cleaned their plates.

She then introduced them to some games the monks played. Merels, Foxes, and Geese were favorite pastimes when the cloister was on the church property.

To prevent nighttime mischief, Emmy wanted to find an activity that would keep the boys occupied rather than having them out and about, looking for trouble, as was their habit.

"We might find game boards, as monks often painted or carved them into the wooden or stone bench seats around the building. I expect we'll eventually see some artifacts from the monasteries that disappeared with the dissolution of the Catholic Church. The Rockhurst church became an Anglican church when the townfolk persuaded King Henry VIII to preserve it because of its proximity to surrounding settlements.

"King Henry VIII agreed but destroyed the cloisters, and the land became a cemetery. The King's guards took anything of value back to London to add to the King's coffers."

"What be a coffer, Miss Emmy?" Jeb asked, as he was the most questioning of the boys.

"A coffer is the King's treasury, which holds money he could use as he pleased. He needed money to pay for his wars with other countries. So, he confiscated the Catholic Church's riches."

"Thank you, Miss Emmy."

Laughter and giggles echoed through the lodge. Emmy wasn't sure who had more fun. Joeson volunteered to play, as both games required two players. Mr. Hadden and Emmy kept all of them playing by the rules, which was difficult because they all wanted to win. Finally, Emmy called a halt to the fun, as they needed to get an early start in the morning. While putting the boards away, they heard someone knocking on the back door.

Mr. Murphy came and announced, "Keller and James are here to speak with you."

"Please show them in."

James quickly covered his yawn with his gloved hand. Keller moved forward. "Sorry to interrupt your night, but we thought you should know we have spotted some men on the Rockhurst property. One man got as far as one of the buildings. When he noticed the new locks, he hurried back to where he'd come from. We followed them until they left the estate. Our standing orders are that unless they take something, we may not stop them."

"Would either of you like a drink or something to eat?"

"Thank you," James said, and Keller nodded his approval.

Mr. Murphy walked over to the sideboard and poured two large drinks from the Brandy decanter. He strolled over and handed each man a glass.

"Knowing where they entered the property, we'll be waiting for them as they will come back." James handed his empty glass back to Mr. Hadden, as did

Keller. "We'll continue to be on the lookout. However, I don't think they will return until late tonight."

"We have looked at the green caravan, and we would be happy to use it instead of our hut."

"Mr. Murphy has the caravan keys, and he knows which horse should accompany your new home. I believe any time should be okay for you both to come by and take possession of it." Emmy stood as she planned to walk them to the door.

"Thank you for the refreshments, and please take extra care. The men we saw were carrying guns. We appreciate your loan of our new dry home."

They stood at the door, shook hands, and watched them leave.

Chapter 10

Once again, a new day dawned with clouds obscuring the sun, which had become a usual morning start. Everyone bundled up, as the ride to the village would be cold and most likely wet.

The cook met them at the back door. She handed a large basket to Mr. Hadden. "Don't want none of you be catching a cold. So, packed you warm food and a large pot of tea."

They all walked over to the stout woman and thanked her. She beamed from ear to ear with all the compliments.

Her gestures are a positive sign she approves of our actions. At the very least, I hope that is the case. Servants, in my observation, either adored or despised the people they worked for. There's no middle ground. I hope my positive-thinking attitude will take this endeavor far.

Just as they were ready to leave, James and Keller rode in. " After last night's rain, we thought it would be best to come now to get our home."

"Yes, of course, Joeson will get Mr. Murphy for you. Come back here if we can answer any questions you might have."

The sunlight briefly broke through the clouds, then vanished.

It might warm the building if it lasted, even for a short time.

It didn't take long for Emmy, Mr. Hadden, and the lads to arrive at the village. They rode up to the Stone Cottage. Once inside, they began removing everything layer by layer so they wouldn't miss anything. The lads' intense hard work impressed and surprised Emmy. They seemed to be enjoying what they were doing. As usual, they were competing against each other to find the biggest and best artifacts. They all took a late-morning respite with warm cups of tea and fresh biscuits just as Joeson rode up.

"The green caravan is on the move," said Joeson. "Keller and James were so impressed when they saw the inside of their new home. It sure is wonderful that you are letting them use it."

"I am thankful to the two of them for watching out for us. I believe it is the least I can do."

"Boys, here is a question for you. This work can be tedious and repetitive," Emmy smiled. "I value your opinion on our project."

Eel, of course, spoke first. "I'm looking forward to our findings, so we must work hard."

Jimmy nodded. "It is nice to be away from London. I like it here."

Jeb just grinned. "Me too."

Emmy laughed and announced it was time to return to work so they could find some authentic artifacts. She carefully repacked the basket, leaving their midday meal, still packaged, to one side.

Earlier in the day, Jimmy had christened the decorated caravan 'The Flower.'

When Emmy placed the basket in 'Flower,' the food was safe from the dogs, as they sat by the door whining. The dogs enjoyed the treats Mr. Murphy sent and wanted more. It seemed they knew an ample supply awaited them. They sat beside the vehicle. When they thought someone was watching, they kept whining. Finally, Emmy called them over to her side.

"You both will get more goodies later." She patted each dog on the head. Her reward was a sloppy lick across her hand.

Later in the morning, Eel ran over with a wooden picture. "Miss Emmy, look what I found."

They had been working inside the building because it was still cold and misty.

"Let us take it outside to see if more light will give us a clue what the picture is."

It appeared to be a single piece of wood on which someone had carved a frame and then created a picture inside it. Dirt and dust covered the image, making it impossible for anyone to distinguish it. Jeb and Jimmy held the sides of the frame. Mr. Hadden, Emmy, and Eel stood back a few feet and looked at the carving from all angles. Neither could make out much more than that the building stood off to one side.

"I'm unsure when or who created this piece of

art. We must wait until we get back to the lodge and clean it. The frame is from the same piece of wood as the picture. I must say, it's been cleverly done."

After Eel noted the map location of the section where he had found the picture, Emmy noted the original location in her book.

"Eel, be sure to shut the door tight on the 'Flower,' or the dogs will get in looking for their snacks."

"Yes, Miss Emmy." Of course, where Eel went, so did Jimmy and Jeb.

They devoured the noon meat pie and returned to the Stone Cottage. Everyone found other items throughout the afternoon, but Emmy couldn't always identify the time frame or who had made them. It would be necessary to wait until she could clean and investigate the items.

Jimmy found a fragment of a medieval stained-glass window depicting Christ holding a glass orb. Emmy dated it to the 14th–15th centuries. Eel found an assortment of keys and locks.

They continue to find insignificant items. Emmy's detailed examination would take place at a later time.

Mr. Hadden suggested to Emmy that they test all the items at the lodge. We'll return those items to the 'Flower' and unload them daily to prevent barn break-ins.

They left the site after securing everything they could. The trip back was again quiet, as they had all worked hard. Emmy and Mr. Hadden noticed people watching them from a distance, but they couldn't tell who they were. After supper, the men agreed to find the guards and devise a plan in case the unwelcome visitors tried to reach the site while they were working.

The 'Flower' quickly found its place in the barn, and everyone helped to move the items to the storage room.

Mr. Hadden said, "Joeson and I will find James and Keller. We're taking the dogs; therefore, please lock the door. We'll knock when we come back."

"I plan to work on cleaning the few items we brought back," Emmy announced. Out of the corner of her eye, she noticed the boys following Joeson out of the room.

Before she could say anything, Mr. Hadden spoke up. "Miss Highbridge, I'm sure they will follow us. We will watch out for them and keep them safe. However, I would enjoy seeing how you, an expert, handle the artifacts."

"Of course, I can wait. I'll organize our tools tonight. Please be careful on your outing."

The lads were behind the men and tried to stay out of sight. The two men talked with Mr. Murphy. Before leaving, Mr. Murphy secured the house and windows. Emmy hurried up the stairs toward the storage rooms.

I hope we don't find many items at one time. It might be necessary to take a day here and there to do paperwork. I don't plan on hiring any additional help. I don't have a specific timeline for completing our project, so rushing is unnecessary.

She opted to take her time and hoped the men found the guards. She went to bed and dreamed of Mr. Hadden.

Greyson and Joeson enjoyed their quiet walk. The dogs were beside them or ahead until they heard the boys. They darted back to find them. Of course, the lads didn't listen to the men's protest to return to the Lodge, and the men weren't surprised.

"Just remember to follow our instructions," Mr. Hadden stated.

I'm glad it's dark, and the boys can't see me. He smiled, somehow keeping from laughing. I knew they would follow us.

"All of you are to stay with the dogs," Joeson announced in a stern, deep voice. "If I call the dogs to assist me, you are to hide. Do I make myself clear? This is not a game."

They all hurried to the site, not noticing anything unusual. Suddenly, the dogs started growling low, which first alerted Joeson. He moved toward the enormous animals and finally saw what had gotten their attention. It was the guards. He tapped Eel on the shoulder and whispered. "Stay here."

James and Keller caught up to Mr. Hadden and Joeson seconds before confronting whoever stood before the 'Stone Cottage.' Together, the four men moved closer to the intruders. Two went around the building, while two moved to the front. They counted to ten and shouted at the trespassers, telling them not to move. Of course, the men ran.

The dogs took off after the thieves. In just a few steps, the dogs caught up to the robbers, bared their enormous teeth, and were ready to inflict damage, forcing the intruders to the ground. They were waiting for a command from Joeson. James and Keller bound the intruders.

"We'll take them to town," James announced. "Could you bring a wagon? I hate the thought of walking to Reed."

"Not a problem. The boys and I will leave now. Mr. Hadden can explain why we were looking for both of you."

The two men sat in the dirt with the dogs close at hand. If the men moved even an inch, the deep growl of the dogs got their attention. Mr. Hadden, James, and Keller moved a few feet away so the thieves wouldn't overhear their conversation.

"Joeson and I came here because we saw someone watching us today. We weren't close enough to see who it was. We decided we should have a signal to tell if it was you or one of our thieving friends. Guess they will never learn?"

"You can count on it. Potts is a wicked and evil person. In most cases, he blackmails the people he wants to control. He threatens to barter his collected information about them if they don't do as he demands. So be careful; he is always looking to gather information about anyone who gets in his way."

"I'll inform everyone, including His Grace, about his business methods." Mr. Hadden shook his head. "Oh, before I forget, the lads know one of the additional guards the Duke hired. His name is Willie. They don't trust him because of his shady dealings in London. Those are their words, not mine."

"Don't worry about him. After the group of new

men ran into all of you, he left in a hurry. Said he had to go back to London." Jason chuckled.

"The boys knew what they were talking about. Must admit, I'm not surprised." Mr. Hadden smiled.

"I just remembered I've got a large white scarf. " We'll wave it like a flag if we see you out and about," Keller announced. "James and I stay together. It isn't smart to be alone with these armed men coming and going in the dead of night or even in the daytime."

The cart came into view. "Miss Highbridge heard us. She asked if you would mind taking the men to town in Potts' cart, along with his pitiful donkey, before he eats everything in sight. His latest is that he is eating the wooden rails on this stall."

"Be happy to do so," James grinned. He bound the thieves' hands to the underside of the seat. Keller rode his horse behind the cart to ensure the men stayed in place and to check for any accomplices along the route to Reed. They looked like a parade traveling down the road.

The lads jabbered with Mr. Hadden the entire way back to the lodge. Joeson played with the dogs, throwing sticks for them to retrieve. They enjoyed their reward for standing guard.

I can't stop thinking about Emmy. In my quiet way, I am becoming more attached to her every day. She is honest. Her courage is unmatched by any other woman I have ever known. She cares about people, regardless of who they are, and treats them with kindness and respect, showing a genuine

interest in their lives, past and present. Now I must muster the courage to say something to her. I realized over the past few days that I have been falling in love with her.

Chapter 11

Plopping down on the edge of the bed didn't stop Emmy's thoughts.

I find I'm always watching Mr. Hadden whenever he's near me. He is calm, rarely speaks, and never misses what is happening around him. I find it tiring to keep calling him Mr. Hadden. Would he think I'm too forward if I suggested using our first names while we're in the village or working on artifacts?

All previous thoughts fled her mind as Emmy was asleep seconds after she crawled into bed.

As the sun rose the following morning. Emmy went to the barn and loaded the lads' cart. She and Mr. Hadden determined the best use of their resources would be to include the lad's cart in daily operations.

Just then, the three boys came bounding into the barn. “Miss, can we go with Joeson to see the new puppies?” Eel stood next to her as Jimmy and Jeb gathered around her.

“Please have Joeson come and see me.”

While shouting that he’d find Joeson, Jimmy ran off; the other boys helped her load the cart. Just as they put the last item in and tied it all down, Joeson, Jimmy, and the dogs burst through the open barn door.

“Miss, you wanted to see me?” Joeson’s smile conveyed he knew what the boys were hoping to do this morning.

“Yes, if I’m not mistaken, there are new puppies at the manor house stables. It appears the boys would like to see them.” Emmy smiled. “However, it’s up to you. I know new mothers don’t always like to show off their new families to strangers.”

“You are correct,” Joeson grinned. “But these puppies are four weeks old. I don’t believe their mother will mind, as it isn’t her first litter. I’ll make sure nothing happens to our helpers.”

Mr. Murphy approached Emmy. “Morning, Miss. Cook sent me to ask when you would like breakfast?”

“At the usual time, and if the boys and Joeson aren’t back, we’ll eat without them. They want to see the newest addition to the Rockhurst canine family.”

Emmy, Mr. Hadden, and Mr. Murphy laughed as they watched the boys jabber with Joeson as they left for the manor house.

“I’m not sure I’ll be able to stand the quiet of the

early morning without the noise of the lads." Emmy turned to enter the house just as her stomach growled.

"They'll grow up sooner than you think. Once they're grown, you'll miss the noise and laughter only the youngest can provide." Mr. Hadden sauntered over to stand next to Emmy.

"I know you're right. However, sometimes the lads wear me out."

He grinned, "Me too," as he moved to the back door. "I hope breakfast is soon. This morning, I found I am famished."

They strolled into the sitting room. Now, Emmy decided that this might be an excellent time to discuss using first names. The fireplace brightened the room, giving the usually chilly space a sense of incredible warmth.

"I need to talk to you about something that's bothering me." Emmy clasped her hands and placed them in her lap.

"If I have done something to upset you, Miss Highbridge, I'm sorry. I would never want you to be angry with me. Because…"

"No, no, you misunderstand me. I'm tired of calling you Mr. Hadden, especially when we are the only people in the room. We seem to have a lot in common and enjoy working together."

"I prefer to call you Grey or Greyson, if you have no objections."

He smiled. "I've been afraid you would think me forward if I made a similar suggestion. People think I'm shy and reserved. But I'm neither. I have a demanding father and a spoiled older brother who now wants to tell me how to live. Other names are better suited for them. However, I would never use them in front of a lady.

"My family doesn't care what I think. They never ask my opinion. Just try to tell me what to do. But enough about me. I'm not sure why I just shared all of this with you. I've been thinking about them and us. Thank you, dear lady. I'll consider it an honor to address you as Emmy."

"Do you prefer to be called Grey or Greyson?"

"Now that I think about it, I would prefer you call me Grey."

It seemed as if someone had prepared breakfast on cue. Emmy again wondered if Mr. Murphy had been listening at the closed door. The couple had eaten breakfast by the time the lads and Joeson appeared. Emmy and Grey heard the thunder of the boy's feet and their thunderous voices long before they appeared. Emmy held her flat palm in front of her to quiet them down.

"Stop, one at a time. I won't understand anyone if you all talk at once. Jeb, you go first."

She watched Eel and Jimmy's faces because Jeb rarely spoke first. He talked little because Eel usually had center stage, and Emmy was determined to change that.

"Them puppies be sure some'hing, them even got their eyes open."

Eel exclaimed, "His Grace said we could each have one for our very own. Effing, you approved."

"We'll talk about owning puppies, which will grow to be enormous dogs like Petes and Jerkens." Emmy shook her head.

The boys and I don't know what it takes to own a dog, especially one as large as this.

Once the boys and Joeson finished their meal, they all got ready to leave for the village. As they headed out the door, Mr. Murphy delivered them a large food basket for their afternoon meal, which Grey placed in 'Flower.' The dogs followed, plopped down at the locked door of the caravan, and whined. The boys giggled at the dog's antics. Once underway, the dogs followed behind Emmy.

All the lads would talk about were the puppies and how they looked forward to playing with them as they grew. They all chatted as Eel drove their cart. Grey and Emmy were on their horses while Joeson drove 'Flower.'

The day's work was much like the day before. They found some items. However, most were rubbish or fragments of artifacts. The keep pile remained small. Joeson and Eel burned the garbage pile in small batches, confirming that the items were not worth saving or were just rubbish. The men found the burning pile easy to control, but it made an awful stench that lingered for hours. They deemed it necessary to place the burn pile further from where they were working. The men extinguished the fires and returned to the lodge early in the afternoon.

"Would you boys like to visit the puppies? I'm sure their mother would appreciate you tiring them out again. I also have duties the Duke requires, and you lads can assist me."

"May we go, Miss?"

Eel stood before Emmy. "Maybe we should help

you unload the boxes from today's hunt first."

"No, all of you can go with Joeson. Grey and I can handle the artifacts." Smiling, Emmy looked over at Grey, who was standing close by, and winked.

"What items would you like to bring to the lodge for examination?" Grey moved to the cart.

"Some of these items don't appear to be the type found in a medieval village. I wonder where they could have come from? Now may be an excellent time to examine them."

With Joeson and the lads gone, the quiet that followed their departure pleased the couple's ears, and the silent looks between them were priceless.

As they unloaded the cart, Mr. Murphy came out, pulling a new, long, narrow wooden wagon. "I made this hoping it would help you unload items brought back from the village." He demonstrated how the movable sides would accommodate artifacts of any size. He positioned them right inside the barn door.

"It'll allow any of you to move multiple objects, large or small, in and then convey them to the trophy room. It's narrow enough to fit down the hallway. Hopefully, it will enable you to accomplish more in a shorter time."

"Thank you so much, Mr. Murphy. I'm sure it will make our tasks more manageable."

The six boxes the boys made of scrap wood from the barn sat on the new cart in no time. Inside the boxes were small chests that the boys had found before leaving for the day. Once inside the trophy room, the couple enthusiastically unloaded the boxes. No one had opened them yet, so it felt like they had just discovered them.

They opened each container with care, occasionally needing a screwdriver to open some. The couple scrutinized each piece of jewelry. But something Emmy noticed made her wonder about the trinkets. She believed many of them came after the medieval period.

"Look at this beautiful gold cross. The delicate design features a silver inlay and a clasp on the back, allowing it to be worn as a necklace or a brooch. I found amber beads in the first container I looked in.

"To determine their origins, we must scrutinize items such as keys, earrings, and gold coins. Many people might have collected these items."

Emmy smiled. "We had better get them logged into the record book. The dating of the artifacts will be challenging because of the length of the medieval period.

I'll keep a second record book as my little secret. In case the first one disappears, I'll have a second one.

Grey handed her a box to be placed upstairs in the storage area.

With Joeson and the lads gone, the quiet that followed their departure pleased their ears, and the silent look between them was priceless.

"Later," Grey said. "Did I not see a book we can study for clues about where and when they came from? Determining what year some artifacts are from will prove interesting, as the medieval years encompass a long time."

Emmy took extra care when replacing the objects in the chests from which she had taken them.

Emmy smiled. "I agreed, and we'd best get them logged into the record book. Determining what year some of these artifacts are from will prove interesting." Emmy was cautious about replacing the objects in the chests where they had gotten them. She didn't want to make a mistake.

"There are keys, a mix-and-match of items. From earrings to gold coins, which will require a careful examination of their origins. Many individuals have gathered these items over a long period."

Emmy was cautious about dating the artifacts, as she felt it would be interesting and challenging. She didn't want to make a mistake.

"What years do you consider medieval? Because there is disagreement in England about which years qualify."

"In most educated circles, the years 1066-1485, spanning from William the Conqueror's reign to the end of the War of the Roses, are significant."

"I hadn't realized it encompassed such a long time."

"Yes, this is one of the times when most people disagree. It'll be challenging to pinpoint the exact date of many artifacts."

The sounds of the lads interrupted the afternoon's work. Their excitement showed on their eager faces. Emmy held out her hand, palm facing outward, which meant the lads were to be quiet.

"Jimmy, what did you lads do?"

"Oh, Miss, we got to play with some older puppies, too. Them ran over us, them did. Sure, be fun."

"Can we go see them tomorrow, Miss?" Eel stood next to Emmy.

"You'll have to talk to Joeson. In fact, where is he?"

"His Grace wanted to talk to him about his dogs. We came back by ourselves and didn't get lost." Eel puffed out his chest but forgot to mention that he and his mates had tracked some thieves to their hiding place.

Chapter 12

Early the next morning, the rain beating against the windows woke Emmy. Rubbing her eyes, she stretched and reached for her robe on the bed. After struggling, Emmy scampered over to the windows. The wind drove the rain against the trees' branches, slapping them back and forth, creating an eerie sound. Leaves again flew in circles before they hit the ground.

I wonder if I could go back to sleep. The plans for today will have to change. Going out in the rain and mud is pointless. We would make a big mess at the Stone Cottage.

She dressed, trudged downstairs in search of a cup of tea, and planned to enjoy the quiet while it lasted. Because of the hour, it was only five in the morning, give or take a few minutes. Emmy knew the lads wouldn't be here for a while.

Entering the trophy room, Emmy first reached for the bellpull, hoping someone was in the kitchen.

If not, she could and would make her morning refreshments.

I've been doing for myself for a long time. Emmy sighed. *I find it hard to wait for someone to do my bidding. Since arriving here, I've learned to be a little more tolerant and patient with other people's time. However, sometimes I still forget until I see the look on Mr. Murphy's face.*

Just as she rose from her chair, Mr. Murphy arrived. "Morning, Miss. You are up early this morning."

"Yes, the rainstorm woke me. Once I'm awake, it's time to focus on the day ahead. If possible, might I have a pot of tea?"

"Would you like breakfast as well, Miss?"

"No, thank you. I'll wait for the others to arrive."

Emmy reviewed the items she and Grey had piled in the room's corner last night. Her mind recalled the evening spent with him.

He is a quiet, knowledgeable individual. I enjoy discussing archaeology with him. Grey appears to be as interested in history and its people as I am. I wonder?

Emmy glanced around the room. Items and papers lay in unorganized stacks. Thinking about it wouldn't get it done. She decided to get back to the task at hand. Cataloging the items sitting in the corner from the previous day didn't take long.

Today we'll work upstairs in the storage room to clean, repair, and organize items. It might prove very tedious.

As Emmy cleaned and labeled each item downstairs, she placed them in the hallway so the lads could carry them upstairs. Mr. Murphy came in the meantime and stoked the fire. He left and returned with a fresh pot of tea and some scones, still warm from the oven. The smell made her mouth water.

"Mrs. M. thought you might like a little nourishment, as it is still early for the lads and men to appear."

"Please tell Mrs. Murphy thank you. I've noticed that all the servants who work in the house and on the grounds call you Mr. and Mrs. M. May we address you as such? The formality is very tiring, and I'm different from most people. I consider wonderful servants as important as family members."

"Miss, you all would honor us. Everyone works so hard." Mr. Murphy's cheeks turned a rosy pink as he hurried out of the room.

Emmy became so caught up in her task that she lost track of time. She finished with the new artifacts and didn't notice when the door opened. Grey surprised Emmy when he spoke.

"Good morning. I see you are hard at work."

She turned to look at him with a smile on her face. "Good morning to you, as well. The necklace I found caught my attention, and I didn't hear you enter. I found it when one of the chests fell to the floor. A false bottom existed."

Grey moved, pulled a chair closer to Emmy, and sat down, taking her hand in his. "Our evening last night was most enjoyable. Having time to be with you meant more to me than you'll ever know."

"I, as well. It's incredible how much we have in

common. We are seeking artifacts from previous generations, and you don't mind digging alongside me in the dirt."

"Honestly, I can't explain how much I enjoy myself with you, even in the dirt. I've never experienced such pleasure in any endeavor I've undertaken in my entire life. You have added even more enjoyment with your enthusiasm in every task we do, even the ones I know you don't like."

"Never thought I would meet someone like you. You've started me thinking about a different life than I had planned." Emmy could feel her face warm as she shared one of her innermost secrets with him.

What has come over me? I'm usually not so forthcoming with my thoughts.

"Whatever do you mean, my dear?"

"Did anyone say anything to you, perhaps hint at what Potts and gang sought? I'm only asking if Potts could be after something more tangible, not just a look-see at what is there. In that case, we might face a more significant problem." Grey went over to stoke the fire.

"One man kept a running conversation with his partner the entire time we were with them. Potts believes someone hid a treasure near the buildings, and they are searching for it. One of the townspeople swore some ancestor had been part of a gang called 'The Badder Boys' that had hidden stolen church artifacts long ago. His partner finally told him to shut his mouth, or he would be sure to tell Potts, who would shut it permanently."

Grey turned around and walked toward the fire

with his hands outstretched. "I can't figure out who is responsible or why it would be at the first building. I'm hoping the second building will offer more tangible artifacts. We'll have to see what we find."

The lads' running feet hitting the tile floor announced their arrival. The door flew open seconds before they entered the room, followed by Joeson. Their non-stop chattering shattered the quiet. Emmy often couldn't understand the lads when they were excited because they reverted to the London East End dialect.

Grey walked over and pulled the kitchen bell, alerting the cook and staff that everyone had arrived for their morning meal. The chatter ceased as breakfast arrived within minutes.

Emmy explained, while they ate, how they could address each other when working and living together in the house, including Mr. and Mrs. Murphy.

Joeson frowned. "Miss, I'm not sure I should do that. You see…"

"You and the boys should do whatever you're comfortable doing. I plan to do this only when we are with each other."

James and Keller knocked on the outside door. Mr. Murphy directed them to the sitting room. They knocked on the door and rushed to stand in front of the fireplace.

"I believe the weather is getting worse." Keller rubbed his hands together.

"The weather is why we are still at the lodge. Please warm yourselves, and would you both enjoy some refreshments?"

"Last night, we captured two men trying to enter the building where you have been working. I guess they figured the weather would be an advantage for them. We took them to the sheriff early this morning."

After enjoying a cup of coffee and cookies from the kitchen, the men left and planned to recheck the building later that day.

Emmy announced she was going to the storage area to work on artifacts. Joeson stated he was on the way to the kennels. Eel and his mates, of course, wanted to go.

It might be a good idea to get them out of the house and run off some of their energy. Grey and I would accomplish much more if we weren't constantly bumping into them or answering their numerous questions.

Looking at their faces, Emmy asked if Joeson would take the lads with him. She saw no problem with them going. Of course, that was only if they wanted to go. The answer was the look on their faces when Emmy suggested going with Joeson. They were out the door in an instant.

The day flew by; once the artifacts arrived in the room, Emmy gathered hot and cold water, as well as furniture-cleaning oil, from Mrs. M.

"It be best if everyone had some aprons to cover their clothes." The housekeeper handed Emmy some aprons. "We have many old ones such as these, which I usually cut up for rags. I suggest you return the dirty ones so I can wash them. I don't like to throw any away until they fall apart."

"Thank you, Mrs. M. We all appreciate all you do for us."

Within a short time, they found the artifacts from the previous day on a table.

Emmy gestured toward the table, announcing, "First, we'll start with the encrusted coins."

Grey watched as Emmy poured a generous amount of soap and water from the kitchen supplies into a large bowl.

"Take a few coins and put them into soak. We'll most likely use the brushes on the table to clean them once the dirt is easy to remove. Next, gather up any wooden artifacts. We can clean any finished objects—those varnished, lacquered, or painted with a hard finish—but only if we are very cautious. Too much liquid will ruin the wood. We avoid water on items without a painted finish.

"We use oil, but sparingly. Sometimes, we can use bristle brushes to clean them. I use a small piece of soft cloth molded around a hairpin if necessary. I'll show you what I mean," Emmy showed Grey the different techniques she used to clean the items.

They gathered the wooden objects and divided them into the coating on each.

"Glass surfaces with durable finishes can be wet cleaned, but not immersed. Stone surfaces could be wet cleaned if the exterior facades appear to be stable."

Emmy shook her head when she picked up what appeared to be a letter. "To preserve paper objects like this, one must handle them with special care. If the article is significant, someone will rewrite and salvage the content, though recovering the original is often impossible. Someone will write the translation on a new piece of paper to attach to the original.

"When we finish a few items, we'll place them on the shelves I labeled last night. We'll return the small items in their original containers if they have one. If not, we might create wooden boxes to house them. I have a stack of small cloths to place over the completed items so they won't gather dust, and we will not have to clean them frequently."

Mr. M. delivered mid-day meals and marveled at the objects they were happy to show him, including a clay pot. They cleaned the entire storage area and all unearthed items. One classification could be from the medieval ages, even without specific dates.

She and Grey found they enjoyed holding hands or a silent touch now and then. Emmy watched him work, and he observed her in return. They accomplished an incredible amount of work stress-free with the lads gone.

The couple pushed their chairs closer to the fireplace. Grey placed new logs on the dying fire, as the room had become quite drafty when the temperature outside dropped.

The boys interrupted the couple with stories about the puppies, Petes, and Jerkens. At the same time, Emmy and Grey continued to work. The lads wasted no time after dinner before announcing their departure to bed. Emmy's lack of suspicion and the boys' previous antics vanished beneath her immersion in her work with Grey. She relived the tranquility of the quiet room once she and Grey were by themselves.

At the night's end, Grey and Emmy walked arm in arm to the stairs. Grey put his arm around Emmy, stood, and just looked at her for the longest time. But in reality, it was only seconds.

Emmy reached up and kissed Grey as she put her arms around him. They stood in each other's arms for what seemed a long time, but in reality it was only seconds. Finally, they both ended up laughing.

They silently walked up the stairs to her room. Emmy reached out and kissed Grey when she reached her door. "My dear, sweet, wonderful man, good night."

Grey took her hand, gently squeezed it, and turned toward the stairs. "I'll see you in the morning—sweet dreams, my dear."

So engrossed in each other, neither of them noticed the dressed boys watching from Eel's bedroom door. The lads were ready to bolt downstairs and head outside. The hunt was on.

Chapter 13

Shimmering brightly on the horizon, the sun and a crystal blue sky perfectly depicted the early morning. Emmy couldn't have been more pleased when she peeked out her bedroom window and saw no clouds.

They loaded the cart last night, allowing them to leave early for the village after their usual breakfast of eggs and baked biscuits, accompanied by homemade preserves. Emmy observed the lads and decided they looked tired. They went to bed earlier than she did, yet they seemed to be dragging their feet.

Petes and Jerkens were glad to run with Joeson, Emmy, and the boys. The lads, of course, were happy to be on the hunt. Emmy and Grey were delighted to be together. Grey drove the caravan to the second building, which surprised the lads.

Emmy called a meeting to offer instructions about her new plan. "Grey, Eel, and Jeb will work together at the Stone Cottage. I'll be working with Joeson and Jimmy at the Farmhouse. Our search will be more effective if we work in both buildings simultaneously."

"Miss Emmy, what does simul… that big, long word mean you just used? I neber heard that word before." Jeb asked.

"You mean simultaneously?" Jeb nodded his head and smiled. "It means at the same time. We'll work in both buildings simultaneously."

"Thank you, Miss Emmy. I done learned a new word today."

"It'll take too long to clean up one building at a time because of all the mess they somehow seem to accumulate. We need to find something substantial, or worth keeping, or the Duke might consider stopping the excavation."

Emmy and Grey cleaned a place in the Farmhouse for a small table, which Joeson had fashioned from pieces of wood he had found. They would work inside if the weather became cold or dreary, or move the table outside if the weather cooperated.

In no time, everyone was hard at work. Emmy laughed at the lads, recalling their competitive spirit, which would drive them to work hard to outdo one another.

"Miss Emmy, look what I found," Eel shouted out.

Before she knew it, the hilt of a sword stood before her. Only half of the blade was present, and upon inspecting the edges, many stones decorated the attached sword hilt. Whether the stones were just rocks or precious stones would require extensive cleaning because of the encrusted dirt.

"Oh my, I'll log it in the book while you put it in the wagon, so later we can place it under lock and key."

"Miss Emmy, look what I found!" Jimmy ran forward.

She pointed to the table. "Please set it here so we can examine it." Once on the table, Emmy logged it into the book.

"This is called a conical helmet." She pointed to the piece of the helmet attached to the forehead. This is called a nose guard. They could have used this during the 11th and 12th centuries. Great find, Jimmy."

It didn't take the boys long to convince the adults they needed a board mounted on the Stone Cottage wall to tally their finds. They wanted to track who found the most items. Grey and Joeson mounted a board next to where Emmy was working.

The boys used a nail to draw a line under each item corresponding to their names. Emmy and Grey enjoyed their banter and promised they wouldn't object unless it got out of hand.

The day went by fast. In no time, the Stone Cottage stood empty. The entire group went in and swept it out with brooms. Emmy made the tallies on the board match when none of the lads were looking. They would reward the boys for their hard work upon their return to the lodge.

Emmy announced. "We'll all be working at the Farmhouse tomorrow. I can't believe we finished the Stone Cottage in one day. I thought it would take a couple of days. Everyone worked so hard. Thank you."

To her trained eye, she felt the Farmhouse was more organized: inside the walls, someone had stacked baskets. The items seemed to have some order, unlike those at the Stone Cottage, which seemed messy and disorganized.

As they gathered their supplies to return to the lodge, Joeson approached Emmy. "I'm planning to go hunting in the morning. I thought it might be helpful for the lads to join me. Because they lived in London, they might find it exciting and would also teach them how to hunt."

In the early evening, Emmy laid out the plans for the next day. The impromptu meeting set the tone for the coming day and had become a nightly event.

"Joeson is planning on hunting early tomorrow morning. If you lads would like, you are welcome to accompany him."

The boys' faces showed their excitement, but they didn't say a word. To Emmy and Grey's surprise, they all sat in their chairs, not saying a word.

Looking at them, Emmy frowned. "Don't any of you want to go?"

Sitting next to Eel, Grey tapped him on the shoulder. "Have you, the spokesman, nothing to say?"

"We be just surprised." Jeb grinned.

"Jimmy, what say you? Are you interested?" asked Grey.

Eel jumped up from his chair and said, "Count me and the others in."

Joeson smiled. "We must be up before dawn, for the animals will forage for food very early. I'll be at the back door at four in the morning. Please eat something before we meet, but refrain from bringing any food. The animals would smell your food and disappear. Then we won't be able to find them."

"Yes, Sir, and thank you." The lads said it in unison, then giggled.

"Joeson and I are going into Reed tonight. We are hoping to pick up some information."

Grey reached out, grabbed her hand, and squeezed it. She sighed and touched his other arm with her free hand.

The men departed for town. The lads stayed long enough to help Emmy take the artifacts upstairs, then announced they were off to bed.

Emmy planned to seek out His Grace within the next few days and visit his incredible library for any additional books on the medieval years. Her mind was reeling with all her tasks. She wondered if some of her responsibilities hadn't surfaced yet and shuddered just thinking about it.

Once the house quieted, Emmy went to the trophy room and sat near the fire after covering her legs with a lap robe.

I'm going to change the name of this room to 'Workroom One' because most items will enter this room before proceeding to any other area in the lodge.

The night plunged into coolness, dropping the room temperature—a usual occurrence at this time of year, according to Mr. M., who added more wood to the fire.

He was gone, but a few minutes later, he returned, informing her that two visitors had come to see her. He handed her two calling cards. She didn't recognize either name.

"Place them in the sitting room. I'll be along presently."

Emmy put her pistol in her pocket. She waited until she was sure they were in the room and then ambled in.

Opening the door, she announced her arrival. "Good evening, gentlemen. I'm unsure why you are here. I'm afraid I don't recognize your names."

She motioned them to sit in the chairs near the fireplace. She took a chair directly across from them.

The first man cleared his throat. "I'm Patrick Carton, President of the London Archaeology Society, and my colleague is Bracken Fitz. It has come to our attention that you will be excavating a historical site in the immediate area."

It didn't take them long to hear about my work. I, Emmy Highbridge, will assume control. They will not oust me or sideline me — not this time. This is my site.

Emmy had no intention of telling either of these interlopers what she was doing at Rockhurst. "Well," asked Mr. Fitz, "have you nothing to say for yourself?"

"Actually, I do. I'm not sure why you came without an invitation. I'll be asking you both to leave."

"Miss, you don't understand. Excavation work is

not suitable for women. You must know it is beyond your comprehension how to be successful in this type of endeavor."

Mr. Carton said, "We are asking you to step aside. We are better qualified than a mere woman."

Emmy stood. "I'm going to say this only once. Leave and don't come back. You and your ilk aren't welcome. I'll not argue my qualifications with mere men." Emmy took two steps closer to the door.

"We shall see; we plan to discuss this with Duke St. George. We believe he might know something about this project." Mr. Fitz said, and then stood, as did Mr. Carton.

Mr. Carlton moved closer to Emmy with clenched fists but stopped when the door swung open.

In a clear, authoritative voice, Mr. M. said, "Gentlemen, I'll be pleased to show you to the exit."

Emmy saw the men moving toward the door. She turned and walked up the stairs to her room.

Greyson and Joeson were leaving the Duke's property when they saw James and Keller. However, neither group acknowledged the other. The men rode down the road, always alert to everything around them. Grey and Joeson were sure Potts' men were watching them.

The two men rode directly onto Main Street in Reed. Joeson went to his family's home. It became essential to ferret out any new information. Greyson first stopped at the general store to pick up some supplies, then continued to the Black Feather Pub.

The men stopped talking when Grey entered the room, which didn't surprise him. Sitting at a table after getting his drink from the bar, he noted that the bar noise level returned to its previous volume. Grey lingered over his drink as he watched the action in the room. He was getting ready to leave when Potts marched into the room, greeting people as he moved around.

He shuffled over to Grey's table and sat down. "Evening, Mr. Hadden. How are you?"

Grey tried not to wrinkle his nose as the man smelled like one of London's worst back alleys.

"I'm doing well, thank you for asking. How are you?"

"I done discovered some interesting information about you, my boy. Care to be knowing what it is?"

"Actually, no. But I'm sure you'll be telling me."

"Gots that right. I done had a meeting with your father and brother recently. Can't be saying I liked either of them. That ain't my point. They are looking for you and can't seem to find you."

Grey leaned back in his chair. *I'm sure I know where this is going, but I will let him play out his hand.* "And your point is?"

"Well, I needs your help. If you want to stay hidden from your family, you will assist me, or I'll invite them to my humble town. You do know this is MY town. I think you get the drift of my plan without me laying it all out in great detail. You've got three days to come here so we can settle on an agreement." Potts stood and sauntered away.

Grey shook his head. *Is it time I stand up to my*

family? I will end their foolish games once and for all. I should have done so years ago. He left and rode over to Joeson's family home.

When he entered, Joeson said, "Wait until you hear the latest news."

"I don't want anyone to overhear us. Wait until we are riding back to Rockhurst."

I have some thinking to do, including making tough decisions. I won't let Potts or my family dictate what I do with my life. It's time I took a stand. I'll not leave Emmy by choice; I'll leave that decision to her after I declare my love.

None of this would be easy for him. His idea of dealing with difficulties with his family had always been to ignore the problems and the people involved. Until now, the issues have usually resolved themselves, which has worked out well so far.

Once the town was far behind them, Joeson started his story. "My family has been trying to gather information about Potts and his mates. My father met with a few townspeople after Potts sent someone to hire them. Because of an old injury to my father's hands and back, it is simple for him to refuse Potts and his gang. They know I work at the estate and suggested that my father get me to leave, as there will be big trouble soon."

"Did they tell you by chance how soon this would happen?"

"No, my folks have been noticing a rough group of newcomers in town. I don't think we have much time. People are estimating only two weeks, maybe less.

"We'll have to think of a way to outsmart them." Grey made two decisions. The first to have a natter with Emmy. At that moment, he realized he loved everything about her and had no intention of losing her. Emmy was his answer to his prayers. His second decision was to discuss the latest developments with the Duke upon their arrival at the estate.

Riding their horses to the manor house, Joeson dismounted and pounded on the door. Grey wondered if they would wake His Grace. His fervent wish was not to. However, they needed to plan, and the sooner, the better.

Holding up a lamp, William, the butler, opened the door just enough so he could peek out into the night. Once he recognized Joeson's voice, he invited both men into the foyer. Greyson cringed when he noticed the scowl on the man's face.

"Do you know what time it is?" The butler growled.

"Yes, William, but we must see the Duke tonight. It cannot wait until morning."

They all turned toward the staircase when they heard His Grace's footsteps on the stairway. "I'm sure this is not a social call. Let's move into the sitting room. You both look like you have ridden some distance."

The men stood silently as they waited for His Grace to join them.

Once the Duke stood beside him, he turned to the butler. "William, you may return to your bed."

Watching the butler leave, he motioned for Grey and Joeson to enter the room with his hand. His

Grace closed the door behind them. The fire was still burning, so the room was semi-warm. Joeson walked over to the woodpile and added a couple of logs.

"Not to worry, gentlemen, I wasn't in bed. Just sitting in my favorite chair, reading before the fire in my room. Thank you, Joeson, for adding some wood to the fire. What are you doing here at such a late hour?"

"We went to Reed tonight to gather any new information. Joeson went to his parents' home and received disturbing news. We need to develop a plan. Otherwise, there's no telling what will happen."

After hearing Greyson's story, the Duke stared at the two men. "Do either of you have any suggestions? Nothing is worth our lives. However, I'll not let a thug dictate my life. We owe it to Reed and the other towns to stop Potts and his ruthlessness."

"I plan to contact the Roma Camp. Brishen is in charge and a family friend of mine. He'll come to assist us, as he owes Emmy's foster mother a debt for helping to establish the Roma Camp on her property. I would also suggest you contact your son, as I'm sure he'll support Emmy."

"I'll send a message tomorrow to Clay, who can contact the Roma Camp. It sounds like we have little time; we must make some plans of our own."

The Duke stood, which the men took as a sign that it was time to leave.

Greyson spoke up as soon as Joeson left the room. "I spoke to Potts at his pub tonight. I need to follow up on my conversation with him. If possible, could you come to the lodge early tomorrow afternoon? It is vital."

"You can't give me the information now?"

"No, Joeson doesn't need to hear what I have to say, as he might return before I have told you everything."

"I shall be there at two. I have other meetings tomorrow morning."

"Thank you, Your Grace," Grey joined Joeson at the front door. They rode back to the lodge in silence.

Chapter 14

To ensure the lads were up, Emmy knocked on each door. “Are you up and getting ready?” The boys stood in the hallway as she finished, making the rounds to each room.

They couldn’t stand still for a minute, marching up one way and then turning around and marching back. Emmy hid her smile behind her hand.

“I’m not sure who is more eager. I don’t believe any of your feet are touching the ground.” She laughed as each boy looked down at his boots. “Be careful and listen to Joeson. Go down the stairs and get your morning meal. It’s waiting in the sitting room.”

With time on her hands so early in the morning, she went directly to the storage room and cleaned up the wooden picture that Jimmy had found the day before. The images appeared faded, as she expected, but she could still make out the picture. There was no trace of any clear finish or preservative deposit anywhere on the article. Removing the dirt from the curved, rough lines would be tedious work.

Opening the door, Grey cleared his throat. “Morning, dearest Emmy.”

She turned and gave him a radiant smile. “Good morning to you, Sir.” She laughingly bowed her head. “I’d hoped you would come a little early. The boys left some time ago.” She reached out and hugged him. “I met Mr. M. on the stairs, and he informed me that breakfast was ready.”

Emmy and Grey enjoyed each other’s company. It didn’t happen often enough. After breakfast, they held hands and walked up the stairs to the storage area to work. Once they were there, Grey motioned Emmy to a chair. After she sat down, he moved his chair to face her.

“Why are we sitting like this? The work area is this way.” She pointed to the articles on the table. “You are making me nervous. Is something wrong?”

“No, I’ve just discovered I have a problem. Please humor me because I’m not sure where to start.”

Emmy placed her hands in her lap. “I’ll be happy to do as you ask.”

“I’ll start at the beginning. If you have any questions, please wait until I complete my narrative. I’ve lived a remarkable life. I left my ancestral home two months ago when my father demanded I marry the young woman who lives next door. My father and brother are seeking her funds to support their lifestyles.

“I rarely argue with my father or my brother, the

heir, because I found it easier to ignore them, which seemed to work until now. They usually gave up on their schemes and left me alone. I should have taken a stand against them years ago. They are drowning in debt because of their gambling habits. To make matters worse, my dear grandfather died a few years ago and left me everything not entailed to the estate or the title of Duke. Because of their heavy gambling debts, they are demanding I give my inheritance to them and marry the chit next door."

Grey stood up, walked around, and stopped next to Emmy's chair. She reached for his hand and held it tight, then he sat down again.

"I never wanted or needed a title. The last time I saw my family, I finally stood up to them by leaving after I told them I would not do what they considered my family duty. They are frantic to find me."

"I don't know what to say. I'll help you in any way I can."

"Potts has hired a group of thugs to come and steal whatever they want. Joeson and I went to inform the Duke on our way home last night. His Grace is sending for his son, your brother-in-law, and the Romas." Grey sat back in his chair and let out a deep sigh. Before Emmy could say anything, he continued.

"Emmy, I've realized I love you in the last few days. It was the moment I met you." He got down on his knee and reached into his pocket. "I've carried my grandmother's wedding ring in my pocket since yesterday, trying to get up the nerve to ask you to marry me. When all this is behind us, will you please consider marrying me? I truly love you with all my heart."

Emmy hadn't moved or said a word. She sat there with her hands in her lap.

"You are not required to answer me this very minute. I know this is sudden, but I must tell you how I feel. You can think it over as long as you say yes." Grey smiled and swallowed hard, hoping to keep his nervousness in check. "I know this probably surprises you, but…"

"All my life, my ambition was to become a well-known archaeologist. Once I discovered my interest in the ancient past, it has been my goal for as long as I can remember. I've ignored all else until you came into my life. Finding someone interested in my chosen occupation is more than I could have ever hoped for. You are interested in my work?"

"Yes, Emmy. I am ready to be your husband and work partner. I…"

"Watching your presence daily since our first meeting, along with your interactions with the lads and anyone else, made me admire you. Since then, I've learned to love the man you are. I want to be your wife and partner. I love you too, you see."

Greyson grabbed her hands and pulled her from the chair, pulling her into his arms. "Will you accept this ring?" He slipped it onto her finger. "This was my Grandmother's wedding Ring. If it is too old or not grand enough, I'll buy you another."

"Wearing your grandmother's ring for my entire life would be an honor. It will become the Hadden family ring."

Emmy couldn't believe the size of the center

diamond. It sparkled and changed hues as she moved her hand. Smaller diamonds graced the key stone, and the ring band featured smaller diamonds.

"I want you to understand I didn't ask you to marry me because of my family's plan. I asked you because I love you and your commitment to me. Nothing, including my family, will stand in our way of a life of happiness."

Chapter 15

The door resounded with a knock. Mr. Murphy walked in and announced lunch was waiting for them in the sitting room. “Cook felt you might like something to eat as you ate breakfast early this morning.”

“Please tell her we appreciate her thoughtfulness. I suddenly realize I’m hungry.”

Emmy smiled as they followed behind Mr. M., holding hands. The couple had no sooner sat down when Mr. Murphy returned to announce the Duke’s arrival. Emmy hastened to make a place for him at the head of the table moments before he entered the room.

“How did you know I hadn’t eaten yet? People at the manor house are always trying to regulate my food. My dear wife seems to be the ringleader, as she has recruited the entire household to spy on my eating habits.” He chuckled.

Moving to the sideboards, they gathered their

choices, sat at the table, and discussed the recent finds from the medieval site. After the maid removed the dishes, everyone enjoyed a cup of tea and sat around the fire on another cold day. His Grace informed them he had sent messengers to his son, Clay, and the Roma camp at daybreak.

"Before we go any further, we must discuss Emmy's unwelcome visitors last evening."

"Who is he talking about, Emmy?" Grey reached for her hand.

"Two men from the London Society of Archaeology came to say how inadequate I was to be working on an excavation of this importance. I was rude and told them to leave and not return. Mr. Murphy was more than willing to show them the door."

His Grace shook his head. "I wouldn't talk to them. I've never met two of the more pompous, self-serving men. They hoped they could stay at the manor house to discuss the evacuation. Believe me, they left within minutes of arriving. I don't think they will return, but don't worry if they do. I'll again send them on their way."

Greyson explained Pott's blackmail scheme. After much discussion, all agreed that meeting with Potts was too dangerous for Grey. His Grace didn't take long to notice the ring on Emmy's left hand. Greyson explained their plan, and he asked him to keep it a secret.

"I would suggest Emmy put the ring on a chain around her neck because other people will notice, just as I have. May I be the first to congratulate you both and tell you I'm pleased with your decisions?"

Seizing this opportunity, Emmy took his Grace to the storage room to show him what they had recently unearthed. Seeing the objects was more impressive than talking about them. The jewelry was clean, the sword's hilt's semi-precious stone sparkled, and the helmet was exceptional. Emmy recognized his disappointment at the small amount.

Potts' actions suggest he anticipates more than he reveals.

Emmy walked his Grace to the back door and then searched for Grey, who had disappeared when the Duke mentioned he was leaving. She found him sound asleep in one of the chairs in the sitting room. Emmy knew if she sat next to him, she wouldn't be awake for long. All this intrigue made her tired.

Emmy heard the lads just as they scurried in the back door. She strolled into the hallway, expecting to see their excitement. All she saw was gloom and doom.

"What is wrong with all of you? Didn't anyone have any success hunting? You look like you lost your last friend."

"We decided we don't like hunting. The animals are what be the word, Joeson?"

"I think you mean regal?"

"Yes, regal. We not be going ever again." A deep frown creased his face. Then he made a face and closed his eyes. "It be awful."

"What if you don't have anything to eat? What then?" Emmy kept a straight face.

"If we must, we must, but not if someone offers a choice." All three lads nodded their heads after Eel spoke.

"If you go into the sitting room, I'll have Mr. M. bring you something to eat."

"Me thinks we should change our clothes first," Eel announced, holding his nose.

"Great idea. I'll do the same and join all of you for lunch." Joeson watched the boys run up the stairs. "They liked the hunt, not the killing or the gutting of the animals."

"They didn't cause any problems, did they?"

"No, they were most helpful. However, the lads told me in no uncertain terms that there is no need to ask them to go hunting again." Joeson chuckled as he shook his head.

"Thank you for giving them an experience I believe they will never forget."

Emmy strode into the kitchen rather than ringing the bell. Mr. and Mrs. M. sat at the table, enjoying what looked like tea.

"Please excuse me. The lads and Joeson just returned from their hunt. According to the lads, they would like to eat. Could you bring some food to the sitting room? They have decided never to hunt live animals again. Living in London, they never learned the harsh reality of where meat comes from. It was a rude awakening for our lads."

Chapter 16

Emmy went to the storage area and began perusing the artifacts again.

There isn't much—only a few odds and ends—which makes little sense. When I read over the diary. The writing talks about a large village. Two prominent stone buildings featured slate roofs. There had to be some storage buildings, but how were they used? When were they built? There are many questions and few answers at this point.

Something is off. I just can't put my finger on it. Thatched-roof house remnants imply they were on the main village road, but eventually disappeared. Someone constructed the stone building later. It puzzles me to think Potts would risk his life for a few trinkets. There has to be something more.

I sure hope time is on our side. I believe we will have completed our project by the end of next month.

"Miss Emmy, can we play our games up here?

We don't want to bother Mr. Grey. He be sleeping," Eel said as he and his mates walked into the room.

"Of course you may. I like to hear your voices. I'm glad you are enjoying the old games."

"We gots only three players. Would you play a game or two?" Once Jeb finished talking, he started biting his nails.

"Yes, Jeb, I would be happy to do that." She reached over and touched his fingers as she shook her head.

All the boys settled at the only table not covered with artifacts. They played Commerce, which was Emmy's favorite. She kept the game scores to prevent the boys from cheating. Laughter filled the room, which was music to Emmy's ears.

After a few hours, Emmy finally stood and said, "I must get some work done. All of you look like you could fall asleep at any moment."

For once, they didn't argue, just hurried off to bed. Emmy wondered if they were up to something because they always tried to find a reason to stay up longer, using one excuse or another. After all, the London nighttime was when they were out and about on the hunt, as they always said. She promised herself that she could check on them before going to bed.

She had just started cleaning a new carving when Grey knocked on the door and entered. "Guess I took a long nap. Sorry."

"I almost joined you. The boys ate a small meal, but not much."

"Most likely, hunting is still not sitting well with them. Sometimes, I forget they are not grown-ups and are from London."

"According to my sisters, they are very resourceful young lads. Every time a significant family problem occurs, they are right in the middle. They have no fear. I worry about them."

"I'm sure they do not know Potts is trying to blackmail me because we didn't talk about it while they were in the house. We must discover Potts' plan to attack the lodge and excavation sites. Perhaps Joeson can visit his family tomorrow and see if they are aware of anything new."

Hand in hand, they went downstairs to sit before the fire. It was a peaceful place, and they knew it wouldn't remain this way for much longer.

The boys looked rested the next morning when the couple found them in the sitting room—the lads who missed nothing kept giggling. Once or twice, Emmy touched the ring hidden beneath her collar. The lads kept snickering. Emmy raised her eyebrows at them, and they smiled so innocently. They didn't fool Emmy for a moment. She knew they were up to something.

Mr. M. strolled in. "I'm sorry to disturb you at breakfast. We have a four-legged visitor trying to get into the barn. I'm sure he is looking for some food." He didn't smile, but Emmy saw the twinkle in his eyes.

"I'm sure you are talking about Potts' donkey. We never found out his name, did we?"

"No, Miss. However, I must say he looks in better health." Mr. M. chuckled.

"Some of our plans will have to change for the day. Joeson, please take the donkey back to Potts and tell him, 'I'll sell the animal if he returns.' Also, please talk to your parents to see if there is any news about more new arrivals in town."

"Yes, Miss. First, may I have my morning meal?"

"Of course," Emmy chuckled. "I wouldn't want you to starve."

"Miss Emmy, we not been to Reed yet. Might we go with Joeson?" Eel quickly added.

"It is up to him if you boys can accompany him."

"Yes, Miss. I would appreciate the company. It is not a long trip, but the scenery never changes much."

"You lads, listen to Joeson. Reed is not a friendly place for people living on the Rockhurst Estate, especially those in the lodge."

In unison, the boys said, "We be promising to listen to Joeson."

"I would like to ask you to purchase some fencing and some other wood to reinforce the windows in the buildings. I shall write you a list," Grey reached for his cup. "If the lads have no objection, I suggest they drive their cart to Reed. Once we have completed our work, I want to restore the Rockhurst estate to its original appearance."

"Grey, what an excellent idea. I'll see if I can find a drawing or diary that might provide an idea of what the area looked like in the past."

The lads and Joeson left to get the transport for their trip. Grey and Emmy watched them as they headed to the main road out of the estate. Once they made a sharp turn, they were out of sight.

They hadn't gotten far when a stable hand flagged them down. "His Grace requested you come to the manor house now."

"I'm on my way to Reed. Did His Grace say why I must come immediately?"

"Yes, something is wrong with two of the dogs. Neither of them should be having their pups for a month or more."

"I am afraid I must go straight to the kennels."

Once they arrived at the kennels. Joeson got off his horse and walked straight to the boys. "I'm afraid we'll not be going to Reed. I must stay until the dogs are out of danger."

Eel blurted out, "We can go to Reed, get the supplies, drop off the donkey, and come right back."

"I don't know what Miss Emmy will say. I–"

"Hurry, Joeson, the Duke wanted you to report to him sooner rather than later."

Joeson walked up to the lads still in the cart. "See you back at the lodge. Be careful while you are in Reed," Joeson ran behind the stable lad.

Traveling to town posed no problems for the lads. The trip was uneventful. All they had to do was follow the signs to Reed. Few people were on the road, and no one seemed to notice them as they traveled or upon their arrival in town.

"Now be our time to help Miss Emmy and Mr. Grey? Did you see them holding hands?"

"I did last night when we listened to them

talking." Jimmy slapped Jeb on the back.

"Me too." Jeb giggled.

Stopping in front of the pub, they all went inside. Eel talked to the man at the door. "We be looking for Mr. Potts. We done gots his donkey tied behind our cart."

The big man said, "You be waiting right here. Don't move."

The three lads looked at each other. Eel shrugged his shoulders. Within a few minutes, Mr. Potts came stomping into view. They had only seen him from a distance, but all three of them noticed how everyone got out of his way as he walked away from the bar towards them.

"How about you, fellas? Tell me why you have my donkey?"

"He done come all by himself to the hunting lodge at Rockhurst. It seems he be liking it there. Miss Emmy said her would sell him if he comes back." Eel turned to leave, and his mates followed him toward the door.

"Wait, what be your hurry? I appreciate you all coming and bringing the dumb animal back." He pointed to one of his men. "Toothless, get the senseless animal and put him in his stall. Tie the fool to the rail so he can't run off again. How about a drink, boys, and some food after your long trip? I would like you to answer some questions."

"We got errands to do."

The lads hurried out before anyone could try to stop them. It was easy to find the general store and get the supplies Grey requested. The trio hoped to find out what was happening because something was afoot. It wasn't something they could explain. It was the energy flowing around them. The lads always listened to their instincts, which never let them down and often kept them out of trouble in London.

Driving the cart down the street, they tied the horse to a hitching rail and walked back behind the pub so they could listen to the men's conversation. It wasn't long before they figured out what Potts was doing.

"It is time to leave so we can warn Miss Emmy and Mr. Grey."

Eel turned to lead the way when three men reached out to grab him. He and Jeb twisted away. Jimmy tripped on a large bucket and fell, hitting his head on a large boulder. Before his mates could go back and help him, two of the men grabbed Jimmy's arms and dragged him in the opposite direction.

The two lads followed close behind, yet hidden from the men's view. They saw them push Jimmy into an old, dilapidated building. It wasn't far from the pub. Locating some large rocks and sticks, they started throwing them at the structure. One man came out and tried to catch Jeb. He threw a rock and hit the large man on the head, knocking him to the ground. Eel found a piece of twine, tied the man up, and stuffed a dirty rag he saw on the ground in his mouth.

"One down, two to go." Eel grinned at Jeb.

A man came around the building, and the boys froze in place. "You be working at the hunting lodge?"

Eel nodded his head. "Them men took our friend and are beating him. We be going to rescue him."

"You must be the three lads Joeson mentioned. I'm his father. Here is what we are going to do." The man went to the road, let out a whistle, and four men materialized. They went to the back of the building and opened the door. Before Potts' men inside could react, they were on the floor, motionless. Joeson's father, with the help of a second man, picked up Jimmy, who was unconscious.

"Our cart be missing." Jeb poked Eel.

"Not to worry, young man. Joeson drove your cart on one of their recent trips home. Once I recognized it, I came looking for you and hid it from Potts. Don't think he is smart enough to find it."

CHAPTER 17

Emmy had been working side by side at the Farmhouse with Grey during the morning hours. They had taken a mid-morning break, eating some fresh scones, and drank some delightful, refreshing tea. The note attached to the cups told them the tea was the cook's specialty. They sat as close as possible without Emmy sitting on Grey's lap.

Much to Emmy's delight, she found an herbal book among other items in excellent condition in the Farmhouse. At first glance, she discovered drawings of plants, along with a description of how to use them for healing. They took a short walk outside and were delighted to hear birds singing and the occasional sound of an animal scurrying around in the bushes next to the building.

She turned away from the building when she heard a horse approaching. The dogs ran out to greet Joeson.

"Good afternoon, Miss. I hope I haven't missed

anything important. I had to assist His Grace with a dog problem, and her puppies-it seems they are all coming into the world simultaneously."

Emmy frowned. "Where are the boys? Aren't they with you?"

"No, Miss. Just as we were leaving. I discovered His Grace required my help. The lads assured me they could deliver the donkey and pick up Mr. Grey's supplies. I thought they would be…"

"Oh, Joeson, you should never have let them go to town alone. Bring the horses around. We must hurry to Reed before the lads get hurt or worse."

"I'm sorry. I didn't realize." Joeson hung his head.

"You had no way of knowing. I should have offered you an explanation about the lads always looking for trouble, which they usually find. No point in worrying. Yet!"

Joeson jumped off his horse, ran, and gathered up the other horses grazing a short distance from the Stone Cottage. With each step, Emmy ran toward the building, calling out to Grey.

Before they could gather their thoughts, they were on their way. They pushed their animals to the limit. The horses needed a breather from time to time, and people crowded the road as it neared town.

A man waved them down just as they approached the outskirts of Reed. He moved back among the trees once he realized they had seen him.

The second Joeson recognized the man; he called for Emmy and Grey to stop. The riders dismounted and hurried over to the man's hiding place.

"Don't be turning around. I rather no one sees me talking to you. Your father sent me to wait 'cause he knew you would come, sooner or later." He pointed to Joeson. "The young lads are at your folks' home. One of them got badly hurt. After I leave, you go there. Don't be going way of Main Street. Potts and gang are watching all entrances and exits into town."

They all heard the man leave, but none of them saw him. The shrubs, trees, and underbrush obscured the entire area. Unless someone knew where to look, they would think it impassible.

Joeson said, "I recognized the voice as my Uncle Jordy. He has had many run-ins with Old Man Potts. Uncle moved away from Reed. I wonder why he is here. I'm afraid it means big trouble."

Hurrying to their horses, the trio stayed outside the village and took an old path around Reed. Weeds had overgrown it, and it looked like the rest of the surrounding area. If anyone looked hard enough, they might see their tracks. They hadn't gone far when Joeson dismounted and hurried back to Emmy and Grey.

"Leave the horses here. It is another path not used. I'm not sure Potts is unaware. The animals should be content here for a short time, as there is plenty for them to eat."

They tied their horses to one of the huge tree branches off the rugged trail. Emmy and Grey scrambled behind Joeson, who veered toward another side road—walking past two vacant houses hidden among the bushes and trees. They dashed across the street toward the back of a home. A large vegetable garden was in the center of what appeared to be a backyard.

Beautiful flowers bordered the area, creating a fence alongside the house. Joeson put his fingers to his lips, scrambled up the steps, and knocked on the door, which was in the center of the house. An older woman wearing an apron pulled the door open and motioned for all of them to follow her.

Eel jumped up from his perch on a wooden stool. "Oh, Miss, it be my fault." He stood before her, but his eyes continued to look away from her.

"You have some explaining to do, but this is not the time or the place. Where are your mates?" She gently brought his face up so that she could look at him.

"Jimmy, 'im be hurt bad. The doctor won't come to 'elp 'im." Tears flowed down Eel's face. He pointed to Jeb, who sat on the floor and didn't look up or speak.

"Would someone explain to me why the doctor won't come?" Emmy scanned the room, looking at each adult.

Joe and Sarah, Joeson's parents, introduced themselves to Emmy. They greeted Greyson, having met him on his earlier visit to Reed.

"Well, Potts and I've had many falling outs recently. He has told the people in Reed not to have anything to do with my family or me, which, unfortunately, Potts has included the doctor," Joe said. "So we all stay far away from Potts and his gang."

"I learned never to hate anyone, but I must admit, Mr. Potts is trying my patience.

Occasionally, I aid my older sister in her herbal practice. Perhaps I can help Jimmy. It will depend on his condition."

Sarah stepped forward. "Please follow me. He is in the back storage room, as it was impossible to take him upstairs." The ladies left the room.

The space proved to be little more than a large cupboard. However, a cot large enough to hold Jimmy sat pressed against the wall. Emmy rushed to his side and kneeled on the floor. A blanket covered him; he looked so pale. His eyes were closed, and he didn't make a sound.

"Can you hear me? It's Emmy. I'm here to help you."

Jimmy peered through swollen eyes. "I be glad you be here, Miss Emmy." He moaned.

She reached out and touched his hand to offer some comfort. He flinched, and then she noticed the bruising, which appeared to be everywhere she looked.

By tomorrow, his entire body will be black and blue. I wish I could get my hands on the men who did this.

She shut her eyes and sighed. "You just lie still. I'll clean your wounds. I want to get you back to the lodge. Right now, there is too much of a chance of someone seeing us."

Emmy stood and motioned for Sarah to follow her. They walked back into the main room.

Grey took Emmy's hand. "How is Jimmy?"

"I don't think any of his injuries are life-threatening. I must clean him up first before I can determine his condition. Is there any laudanum available? Jimmy's entire body will be a mass of bruises by morning. He will need something to dull the pain if we move him."

Joeson stood. "All of you must leave in the dark. There is a chance someone will see you. We can create a commotion on the other side of town so you can slip away. Believe me when I say Potts will kill you if he finds you. I hate to think what he would do to us if he caught you here. I have never seen the man so angry."

"Can we get the cart ready for the trip back to the lodge?" Grey motioned for Jeb to sit by him, as it would be hours before they could begin the trip back to Rockhurst.

Sarah told Emmy. "I believe this is what you need."

Emmy opened the small bottle, removed the top, and poured a small amount of reddish-brown liquid onto the tip of her finger. Touching her finger to her lips, she could taste the bitterness.

"I'll not use much. The laudanum will help keep Jimmy comfortable and quiet. Let me clean him up and see to his wounds."

Returning to the room with a large pan of warm water, bandages, and towels, Sarah set them on the floor, as there was nowhere else to put them. The two women quietly got to work, making Jimmy as comfortable as possible.

When the dog started running back and forth to the door, Joe calmed the dog and opened the door. Everyone scurried out of sight just as a man rushed into the house. He slammed the door and ran into the room. Joe introduced him as Jacob, a neighbor.

"Potts hasn't found out about the lads yet." Jacob removed his hat. "We done took Potts' men and deposited them in the abandoned mineshaft. We hope you can safely return to the estate before they find the brutes missing."

Emmy hurried back into the room. Grey came over and took her hands while Joe lit a few lamps.

"There is a possibility Jimmy has a broken leg. I can't tell for sure until the swelling goes down, which might take a day or two. I believe he might have a couple of cracked or broken ribs. Sarah helped to bind him. Hopefully, this will stop him from being further injured when he's moved. To relieve some pain, I gave him a small amount of laudanum. I'll provide him with more when we leave. I don't want him to cry out and give our position away."

Jeb approached Emmy. Tugging on her sleeve, he said. "Miss, he ain't going to die; don't be letting Jimmy die."

Emmy kneeled in front of Jeb. "I believe Jimmy is going to be just fine. He is a sturdy lad and will recover from his injuries. Come sit next to me so we can plan to leave as soon as it is dark."

Once the planning was complete, Sara fed them sliced meat, apple cider, hot tea, and apple dumplings. The men left to gather their horses and the cart while the women prepared Jimmy for the ride. He wore ample clothing, hoping it would protect his body from further bruising. Sara gave Emmy a water container for drinking on the way to the estate, in case it took a while to reach the estate.

Jimmy couldn't walk. The men carried him to

the cart, which they had filled with straw, hoping he would be more comfortable. They made him as comfortable as possible. Emmy gave him another minimal dose of laudanum.

Once they were ready, most of the men left to create a diversion. Joeson and his horse led them away from town, taking another used side path. Eel rode Emmy's horse while she and Jeb stationed themselves in the cart to protect Jimmy. Greyson followed them. The sun hid behind clouds, slowing and complicating their progress. No one could see them, but they couldn't see anyone either.

They had been gone for about an hour when they heard the noise of an approaching rowdy group of men on horses. A band of men was far enough away; no one could understand what they were saying. Emmy crouched in the cart and covered herself and the boys with a blanket. Joeson, Grey, and Eel dismounted. They held the horses' muzzles, hoping to keep them quiet. Their animals were on their best behavior.

Without warning, they heard an animal come from behind them as it burst through the trees and bushes, veering around them and heading right for the approaching group of horses. Emmy moved to a position where he could peer over the cart's seat.

Joeson touched her arm. "I think it's the donkey."

Emmy whispered. "Guess I owe him some food." She moved back to Jimmy as she heard him stirring.

The horses and voices grew loud as they passed them. Emmy and her group waited a long time before venturing any further. They didn't want a slacker to find them. Once they couldn't hear any other sounds, they moved on.

Grey moved along the side of the cart. "I bet Potts and his gang will have guards at the estate's main gate."

He had no sooner spoken when Jeb's head popped up from underneath the blanket. "There be another way onto the grounds. I be sure we can find it again."

Greyson discounted and hurried toward Eel. "Jeb said another entrance exists, and you both know its location?"

"He be right. James and Keller showed us one night when we were going to go to Reed. Them caught us and marched us back to the lodge."

"Eel, I can't believe you three would… I know this is not the time to discuss this, but we will. Do you think the two of you could find it again?" Emmy sighed.

"Not sure," Eel said, hurrying away. "Be pleased to try."

By this time. Joeson had Eel's horse tied up to the back of the cart. "Are you sure, Eel? When there is daylight, everything looks very different."

"What about the cart? We must get it onto the estate?" Emmy touched Eel's shoulder.

"Last time we was here, it be dark, like now. I know we be finding it. Not sure about the cart, Miss Emmy. Jeb, you be coming? We gots to be on foot."

Chapter 18

Before leaping down from the cart, Jeb patted Jimmy on the shoulder. "I be ready. Just go find the water running across the road."

The darkness hid Emmy's tears. "Listen to me, you two. I don't want anyone else to get hurt, do you hear me? So take care." She closed her eyes and said a silent prayer.

Grey walked the boys to the main road's edge. He pointed in the estate's direction. "How far from the main entrance do you think you were?"

Jeb walked out and looked first up the road, then down. "Just be past the bend in the road. Not far first comes the spring and then the entrance."

"Be careful. You know what will happen if they catch you. Call out if you have any problems. Run like the devil if they try to trap you," Emmy whispered just loud enough for the boys to hear her.

Grey stood and observed the boys creep up the road until they disappeared. Suddenly, he heard galloping horses coming down the road toward them. Grey couldn't do anything except withdraw back into the treeline. He hastened back to the cart and whispered a warning to the others.

Grey and Joeson, after discussions with Emmy, decided they would stay hidden in the tree row. They handed their horse's reins to Emmy after she climbed down from the wagon. She whispered to the animals, hoping to keep them quiet.

The two men crawled through the undergrowth. It concealed them. However, branches scratched their faces and hands as the shrubbery tore their clothes. They made sure not to make a sound. The horses and men had not passed them. They could hear them milling about as if they were looking for someone. Suddenly, a loud voice permeated the air.

"What do you mean? The fool fell off his horse. Damn, drunk buffoon. We don't got time for such foolish people. If we don't find the intruders, Potts will punish us. I hate to see Potts angry at us, and I assure you, you don't want to either. Leave the fool here. If we come back this way, we'll pick him up. If not, he can walk back to town. Mount up. We gots to catch those troublemakers."

The horses and riders left the way they had come. Grey and Joeson hurried to the man lying unconscious on the side of the ditch.

"I think they'll be back this way. Let's…"

Eel appeared before the men. "We found it. James and Keller are waiting. They planned to attack Pott's men if they tried to come onto Rockhurst land. Jeb stayed back to warn us if the riders came back. They be clearing a path for the cart.

They all ran back to the cart and mounted their horses. When they told Emmy about the injured man, she insisted they pick him up.

"Miss, he could be a thief or maybe even a murderer, or worse. He could be more trouble than he is worth." Joeson argued.

"You are most likely right. However, I'll not leave an injured man to the elements. It is wrong, and second, my sister would disown me if she ever found out."

Jeb touched her arm. "We not be telling her, Miss Emmy. It be our secret."

"He'll be coming with us. We must hurry."

Their trip to the hidden entrance didn't take long. Joeson and Grey threw the man into the cart. He barely fit. James and Keller appeared; no one spoke. They took a couple of long branches with plenty of leaves and smoothed out the wheel and horse tracks. No one would ever know they had gotten onto the Rockhurst property at this location.

Keller stood watching the road and informed the group that James had gone to tell His Grace of this new development.

James appeared as if on cue. "We are to escort all of you to the manor house just in case the men try to come to the lodge. We have guards stationed in places throughout the property."

They hurried as fast as possible but didn't want to jar Jimmy or the unknown man more than necessary.

The Duke stood at the entrance of the manor house, with the open door behind him. "I have been watching for all of you. Is anyone hurt?"

"Someone badly beat Jimmy. The doctor refused to see him. One of the men chasing us sustained an injury. They left him on the road. I insisted we place him in our cart." Emmy hurried to tell his Gace about all the recent events.

His Grace helped Emmy down from the cart. "I think you all did a magnificent job. Let's get the injured into the house."

A large room at the back of the manor house would serve as the sickroom. Emmy made sure Jimmy was comfortable. He had not awakened during the entire trip.

Potts' man seemed to be coming around and found a place on a makeshift cot across from Jimmy. His words made little sense. He was babbling on and on. Emmy cleaned him up as best she could without removing any of his clothes.

Grey removed two large knives from his pockets. His clothes and boots were mud-spattered. After the dirt dried, she would brush it off as best she could and remove his boots. She checked for broken bones. Only found one large cut on his head near his hairline. After she cleaned the wound, she applied a bandage.

Grey and Joeson tied the man's hands and feet so that he couldn't escape. The group appeared to be dragging their feet as they tried to stay awake. Emmy knew that if she sat down too long, she would fall asleep. Dust still floated around her from the road, causing her eyes to itch, and occasionally she sneezed.

Grey suggested they take turns washing up after

the day's adventure. He would sit and watch Jimmy and their unwanted guest. No one knew his name, so he must have been a hired thug. Emmy took both Eel and Jeb to clean up. She checked them for wounds and or cuts. Before she sent them to the sitting room, she warned them.

"We'll talk about your actions at a later time, maybe as early as tomorrow. You put your life and those of us who came to rescue you in danger. You both think about your actions because there will be a punishment. Now go and sit with Jimmy until I return."

Eel shuffled over to her. "Miss, I really be sorry. We only be trying to 'elp."

"Eel, the word is help."

Jeb reached for Emmy's hand. "I be grateful for you and the others."

Emmy looked at Jeb. "Well spoken, Jeb. Not another word until tomorrow. Now go."

She watched the two lads, who would, in no time, become young men. She shook her head when she thought about what might have happened. Emmy washed her face, hands, and arms and would have loved a bath, which would, of course, have to wait. She returned to the sickroom, found the man wide awake and protesting his treatment.

Keller sat next to him in a chair. "Tell me your name."

"I not be telling you nothing. You know when Potts be finding out, he'll…."

Emmy snickered. "Your friends left you on the side of the road, which does not have many travelers. You could either be there if they came back, or you would have to walk back to Reed. If you aren't aware, a few wild animals still prowl in this area. We didn't leave you to the elements like your friends. However, if you plan to be bad-mannered with your mouth, I'll stick a dirty rag in it. Do you understand me?"

The man's eyes grew large. "Yes, Miss."

"If you need something, just ask."

Joeson entered the room with Petes and Jerkens. They walked over to Emmy and licked her hand.

"I'm sorry. I don't have any treats."

The dogs looked so sad until they saw Joeson hand her something. Their ears perked up as they started sniffing the air. Watching their expressions change as their tails wagged almost made her laugh out loud. Their drool puddled on the floor.

They lay at her feet. When the prisoner moved, the dogs growled.

She laughed. "Good dogs. They won't bother you if you don't move about."

Greyson came back into the room. He brought a chair, a stool, and a blanket. "This is for you, Emmy, because I know you will not leave Jimmy. Joeson and I will watch our prisoner."

The night passed more quickly than they had thought. Emmy woke up twice to check on Jimmy; he was sleeping like a baby. She took that as a good sign. The prisoner, still nameless, continued to watch her. However, she didn't speak to him. Helping a hired predator who was hurt was one thing; being friendly was simple, out of the question.

In the morning, they all took turns eating

upstairs.

Emmy brought some food for Jimmy and their prisoner. She loosened one arm for their uninvited guest so he could feed himself. She fed Jimmy, but his face was so sore that he ate little.

"Miss, my name be Peter Hamlin. Potts hired me to do whatever him needed done. The pay be good, and I only planned to be here for a few days to one week. Then, I be planning to go back to London."

Joeson went out with the dogs and came back laughing. "You'll never guess who is at the barn at the lodge?"

"The donkey wants his food. I promised him last night." Emmy and Joeson both chuckled. "I guess this means we are the proud owners of him by default."

Suddenly, Emmy could hear the voices of adults and children. She listened with great interest.

"My sisters are here with their children. How can that be? It's impossible; I must be hearing things. The Duke sent the messages just two days ago. There is no way they could be here." Then she heard other voices.

"I think I heard Brishen's voice. Why would he be here?" Emmy couldn't and wouldn't leave Jimmy and their uninvited guest. Pacing the floor in the small room didn't settle her nerves. She would have to wait until someone came and told her what was happening.

CHAPTER 19

Appearing at the door, Grey announced. "We have visitors. I'll stay with Jimmy while you go upstairs."

Emmy rushed from the room as she shouted, "Thank you."

Following the voices, Emmy hurried to the sitting room. She stood in the open doorway and couldn't believe her eyes. Her foster parents were the only ones missing. Clearing her throat twice, she finally got everyone's attention. Emmy didn't know who to hug first. The nieces and nephews ran to Emmy the second they saw her.

She picked up Martha, her older sister's little girl, and hugged her. Emmy sat on the floor, and the other three children gathered around, each getting and giving hugs. They were so happy to see her, they all talked at once.

"I'm not joining you all on the floor," Nicola, her oldest sister, stated, giving Emmy her hand to help pull her up.

"It is so wonderful to see all of you. How did you know to come? His Grace just sent you a message and…."

Clay, Emmy's brother-in-law, Earl of Woodhaven, motioned Emmy to a chair. He was married to her older sister.

"How about we all sit down and enjoy a refreshing cup of tea while explaining how we knew to come?"

Just as Emmy reached the chair, she turned back to her sister. "Wait, Nicola, your excellent herbalist skills are required. Jimmy was seriously hurt yesterday. I'm not sure how bad. I did my best to take care of him. Sad to say, I'm not as knowledgeable as you."

"I'm glad you are here too, Barnaby, as I know you will be a big help." Emmy reached out and hugged her sister's husband.

"Along those same lines," Brishen said, setting his empty cup on the table beside his chair. "I heard almost identical information. Emmy, your family has protected mine for years; without them, our Roma band would most likely no longer exist. Your father and mother have been very kind to all of us. We have become one with yours now and forever. I contacted Clay, and we came together. My people are not far from here. We number about twenty-five."

"I had no idea." Emmy frowned. "Most people in town can only do what Potts tells them, or he does evil and mean things to them. When Jimmy received his injuries, the doctor couldn't come to help him because Potts had warned the doctor not to treat anyone unless he approved the treatment."

"The men from our old East England gang are staying in the guesthouse behind the manor house. These men, no longer hardened criminals, gave up their lives of crime a long time ago. Believe me when I say they will protect you and yours with their lives," announced Graham, a long-time friend of Barnaby.

"I'll go see Jimmy in a moment. One of the gang members is in the same room as Jimmy. Please be careful around him. Greyson is there as well. He can fill you in on what happened."

"I'll accompany Nicola." The Duke offered his arm.

"First, I must retrieve my healing bag from the carriage. I never leave home without it." Nicola turned toward the door.

"Please allow me to retrieve it for you," Brishen stated.

Before he could leave, Emmy stopped him and hugged him. "Thank you for coming."

Emmy's sister, Mara, found a comfortable place to sit back and enjoy all the commotion. She preferred to watch and listen. She sipped her drink, afraid she might fall asleep if the room became too quiet. The children went with their nanny to run off their energy.

Clay, Emmy's brother-in-law, stood and paced back and forth in front of the massive fireplace.

"We came before we got your message. The government had obtained a letter from an undercover agent. Telling about a man named Potts, who has been pursuing low-life criminals to help with a problem in a small town.

"Then Graham and Maggie heard that someone from Reed was recruiting men to take over an archaeological site forcibly. Our brilliant minds didn't take long to figure out you were involved.

"As your favorite, best brother-in-law, the one with the wonderful, brilliant mind, we didn't wait for any message; we left that morning, and here we are."

"Barnaby, I did not know you were so…can't quite think of the proper word. Maybe I will later." Said Brishen.

Everyone laughed, even Barnaby. "As I was saying, I heard the identical information. I contacted Clay and Barnaby, and we came together. My people are not far from here. We number about twenty-five."

"I don't know what to say, but I appreciate you more than I can say. To give you a brief history. Potts' men have stolen artifacts from the old medieval village. I'm not sure what he thinks is there. We have found only fragments at this point. Recently, we heard a story about someone who stole items long ago and might have stored them somewhere in the old village. The team almost finished emptying the second building after completing the first one. We have discovered some new sites that we plan to examine when both buildings are empty."

Mara, Emmy's other sister, patted Emmy's hand when her husband, Barnaby, spoke.

"Everyone at the hunting lodge should stay at the

manor house. We'll put a group of men as guards there. I'm sure Potts's men realize you are keeping some artifacts there. Other men will guard the old site. If the thieves are clever, they'll go after both locations simultaneously."

Frowning, Emmy always tried to maintain a positive outlook, but just now found it almost impossible. "What about the manor house? Do you believe Potts's men will try to take us prisoners to make us give them what they want?"

Entering the room, the Duke said, "When all this started, I contacted my friends in London. They will be here no later than tomorrow morning. Rest assured, they can and will protect the estate."

Nicola stood in the doorway while His Grace spoke. Once he finished speaking, Nicola said, "Jimmy will survive his beating. I have seen worse. However, the bruising on his leg is very serious, but it does not appear to have any breaks. He'll need some device to move around, as he can't put pressure on his injured leg by trying to walk on it. Otherwise, he'll drive you all crazy, wanting to be moved from place to place." She chuckled as she walked over to sit next to her husband.

"James and Keller are here for you, Your Grace," said Mr. M. as he entered the room. "They would like to speak with everyone."

"Please show them in."

Mr. M. stood at the door while the two men entered with their hats in their hands.

"Thank you for coming, as I'm sure you bring us some new information." Emmy waved her hands around the room. "This is my family. After you have told us why you are here, I'll introduce you to each member."

James stepped forward. "We thought of barricading the main gate, but once Potts and his gang appeared, they would know we were aware of their plans. James and I suggest we arrange a signal to alert everyone if anyone shows up tonight."

"What kind of signal did you have in mind? By the way, James, it's nice to see you," grinned Clay.

"So, you remember me."

"How can I forget you saved my life on more than one occasion?"

"I would love to hear that story," Nicola said, winking at James.

"Back to business. You can reminisce later," Barnaby said. "We were talking about a signal. Pleasure seeing you, James."

Eel stepped forward. "Jeb got an idea — a good one."

"Jeb, why don't you tell us?" Nicola looked over at the boys standing next to Emmy.

"No, Eel, he should be the one to tell." Jeb glanced down at his shoes.

"It is your idea; you need to explain it." Nicola looked directly at Eel and put her finger to her lips.

Jeb took a deep breath. "We need lanterns. Cover three sides of each one so that you can't see any light. You must attach a small mirror across from the uncovered side. Then, you put a candle in the lantern and light it." He bit his lip and took another deep breath.

"I think," Eel said.

Greyson touched Eel's shoulder. "Go ahead, Jeb.

Tell us what we do next."

"Iffing someone be watching the road, and took the lantern with the light showing through the uncovered side, and swung it back and forth toward the next watch person. The men coming onto the property would not see it. The watch person would only be seeing it." Jeb again glanced at his shoes.

The room was silent until His Grace spoke. "Jeb, you are brilliant. Let us find some lanterns."

Jeb received pats on the back from the entire group. Emmy covered her mouth to hide her smile as Jeb's face turned red. Emmy, Nicola, and Mara went and hugged Jeb. Eel slapped his mate on the back.

"Jeb, let's go tell Jimmy your plan. We don't want to be leaving him out."

The two boys dashed from the room. The men left to find enough lanterns, not knowing how many sentries they would need or how many sentries they would have. Better to have too many than not enough. Brishen went to talk to his people. James and Keller left to keep watch on the main gate.

The three sisters sat and enjoyed visiting while the men and children were gone. Their nanny continued to entertain the children. Before they knew it, the entire group of men was back with all the lanterns they could find.

Joeson produced some usable mirrors. They quickly outfitted the lamps to the best of their ability to match Jeb's description. The men tried it out in the darkroom under the stairs leading to the second floor.

To say it was entertaining to watch was an

understatement. First, one man lit a candle. Then, he ran in one direction, swinging his lantern. The men were working in a small area and couldn't tell if the lamps were working as planned. Once the woman quit laughing at the men's antics. They announced they would show them how to use the lanterns as a signal.

Emmy stood under the stairs, which were dark once the candles in the immediate area were out. Nicola and Mara stood in the hallway. Once Emmy swung her lamp back and forth, both women could see the light. The light was invisible to anyone not in front of her.

Tar would also darken the three sides of the lantern. Mr. M. also mentioned that black paint was in the barn. After deeming the lamps successful, the men, along with Jeb and Eel, left again to locate the paint, as it would be easier to use.

The entire group of men could be in place before it became dark. They set out an early buffet supper of meats, potatoes, and vegetables on the table in the sitting room, since no one knew when Potts and his gang would arrive. They only knew the raid could happen at night or early morning, while it was still dark. The women, minus Emmy, took the children to the second floor. All the women carried pistols to protect themselves.

Just as shadows formed against the trees and the daylight dimmed, Joe, Joeseon's father, and two others from Reed arrived, along with James and Keller.

"We came so we can be of help; you need to tell us where we should go to watch for the gang of ruffians."

Emmy said, "Thank you for your help. We appreciate it more than I can tell you. I'm sure Joe has some information for us."

"I sure do, Miss. It appears Potts and his gang will be here tonight. I believe they are hoping to surprise us. They saddled their horses and left them outside the pub. They might not care much about most things, but they take decent care of their mounts."

"What about the families in Reed, especially the ones Potts threatens all the time?" Asked Emmy.

"Yes, everyone is hiding, including Pott's enemies." Joeson said, "Until we have this under control, the townspeople must stay hidden. Potts could most likely harm them if he knew where they were."

Clay, Barnaby, and Brishen took the time to explain their plan. Brishen and his group would go to the medieval buildings to protect them, while Clay, Barnaby, and their men would take positions near the manor house and the hunting lodge. Once they received the signal, they knew that Potts and his band had arrived at the estate. They would move and encircle them. As time passed, the circle would get tighter and tighter until Potts and his band of cutthroats had to give up.

Emmy felt her archaeological project was responsible, so she stayed to assist at the main entrance to the manor house.

Everyone left for their assignments. Planning to sit on the front porch, Emmy would watch for the sentry lights. She couldn't see the first couple of signals, as the landscape had some small rises before flattening near the manor house.

Hearing or seeing anything from the old village vanished, as it existed too far away, and a small hill shadowed the general area. Brishen promised to send his men to help if others needed any assistance. Emmy was worried about them because they were fearless.

She finally saw a light coming from the main road onto the estate, which meant Potts and his men were on the Rockhurst Estate property; they had arrived.

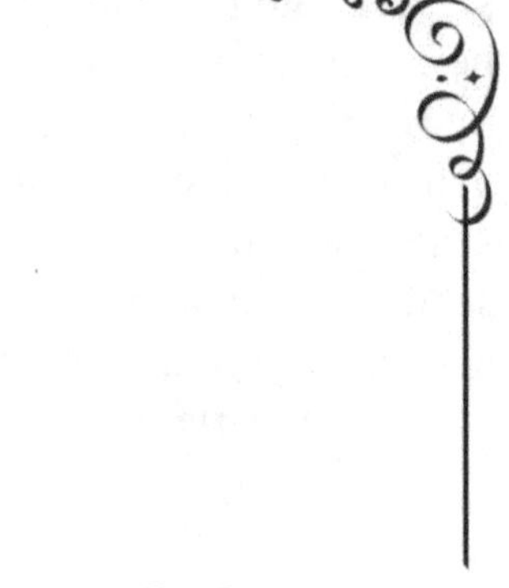

Chapter 20

The sounds of shouting and clashing weapons pierced the evening. A few random gunshots peppered the area. Watching closely, Emmy looked for anyone who might try to slip past the mainline of deference. She slid back enough on the porch so she could remain unseen. Someone would have to come to the main door to see her.

To protect the back entrance, Petes and Jerkens stood guard. Both dogs could easily break the ropes holding them in place if they felt threatened. Mr. M. was behind the back door if someone got that far.

Emmy finally saw movement creeping toward the house. She stood and shifted further back into the shadows. Suddenly, two unfamiliar men, whom Emmy hadn't seen before, appeared, which was perfect because they would think Emmy was an innocent woman they could handle with ease. She removed her whip from her back, uncoiled it, and placed it next to her feet. Emmy made sure there was enough room to use it, as she had a bird's-eye view. The only movement she saw was coming toward the front entrance.

The men's conversation was inaudible, but they were getting closer. Standing precariously still, she waited until they were almost at the porch steps.

"I wouldn't come any closer if I were you."

"You only be a woman, which means you can't do nothing to us. You be our prize for the night."

The first man moved directly toward her voice, but she had moved. He walked up the steps. Waiting until he reached the porch. Emmy flicked her wrist, causing the whip to wrap around his legs, causing him to fall backwards. He lay on his back, moaning. His partner rushed to his side.

"I be coming for you now. Then you be seeing what this be all about."

He never got to say another word. Brishen jumped from behind and knocked him out. He pulled two pieces of rope from his belt and tied both men's hands behind their backs.

"Well, Miss Emmy, we rounded up the men who came to the medieval site. Only ten — a small group — are marching to the lodge. We'll have to wait and see what happens next."

"Thanks for teaching me how to use a whip. I'd never had a reason to use it before. It has come in handy more than once since I've been here."

"It was my pleasure, my dear."

Just about then, the men lying on the ground started shouting insults; they heard men approaching from the main gate area. In time, they saw that someone had secured Potts and his crew's hands behind their backs and tied them to a long rope strung between. Blood fanned across some faces, and their clothing was in poor shape from the fighting. Yet it didn't appear that anyone was seriously hurt.

Brishen and Emmy sat on the porch. In time, Eel and Jeb went to find Nicola to administer medical aid to those who needed care. The only rule was that the intruders would receive care last, unless they were severely hurt. Someone would take all the prisoners to Reed and deposit them in jail. At first light, they would load them into wagons and then transport them to Newgate Prison in London.

It was a long night. No one got to bed before dawn. Nicola, Mara, and Emmy had all taken part in nursing the entire group. Sleeping in shifts was necessary to ensure no one else came to cause any mischief. Potts whined the whole time, claiming the situation was a misunderstanding.

At daybreak, Brishen and his men marched the prisoners to Reed. The townsfolk greeted them with rotten eggs and anything else with a nasty smell. The Romas stood guard until the London guards arrived.

Emmy and her sisters stayed at Rockhurst during the march to Reed. She finally woke up just when the men were returning. Townspeople filed formal complaints against Potts, which they would hand to the magistrate when the time came. The authorities would charge them for the crimes they committed. Because the sheriff was part of the gang, he would also face arraignment.

On the way back to Rockhurst, Grey talked to

Emmy's brothers-in-law about his secret engagement with Emmy. He asked the two men for her hand in marriage so that they could make the engagement announcement in front of her family.

"I think you should get married while we are all here. Emmy's foster parents will be here by tomorrow at the latest." Clay looked over at Barnaby. "Don't you think that is a great idea?"

"For once, I agree with you. I think it's a smashing proposal, " said Barnaby as he slapped Clay on his back.

"Dreaming again, old friend?" Clay laughed. "Grey, you'll find being married to one of the Highbridge sisters will be one adventure after another."

"Wait until Mara and Nicola hear about this; they will be overjoyed. Maybe if all the sisters are married, they will stay out of trouble." Barnaby smiled.

By the time they rode to the estate, they were so tired that they struggled to stay in their saddles. They let Joeson take care of the horses and went to bed.

Emmy shouted out, "Look, the men are up in time for our victory celebration. Your father sent us an excellent roast to enjoy. The Duke and Duchess are coming as well. We have so much to be grateful for."

"Yes, we do, Emmy and Greyson. Would you like to share your news with your sisters? We, Barnaby and I, already know!" Clay grinned.

When Emmy hesitated, Barnaby said, "I don't think I've ever known Emmy to be nervous or speechless about anything."

"Greyson, I believe you talk too much," Emmy said, frowning.

Grey laughed, "Well, I had to ask a family member for your hand in marriage, and this seemed to be an opportune time."

Jumping up from their chairs, Nicola hugged Emmy, and Mara was right behind her.

Barnaby watched all three women with amusement. "Since your foster parents are on their way here. Clay and I thought it would be an excellent idea to have a wedding with all of us in one place."

"I agree one hundred percent." Clay had the biggest smile on his face. "For once, we men knew something before the women." He practically danced around the room. Nicola finally reached out her arm and grabbed his hand to stop him.

Mara tried to give her husband a superior look. "You can wipe that smug look right off your face. Have you forgotten the most essential piece of paperwork required? They need a marriage license."

"Actually, they don't," said His Grace. "I knew about their betrothal a short time ago. Emmy is almost a family member, so I requested a special license from the church. It was the least I could do."

"How did my foster parents know to come? I haven't contacted them." Emmy frowned.

"Oh, I did." His Grace looked pleased with himself as he grinned from ear to ear. "I'm a romantic at heart. Just ask Clay's mother. I'm sorry she isn't here because she is in London; in fact, she has been there for the entire month."

Emmy stood in shock. "I can't believe it. When will they be here? Do you have any idea?"

"I think sometime tomorrow, dear Emmy." His Grace was still smiling.

The sound of running feet stopped their conversation as the lads hurtled through the door. It took Jimmy a few minutes to catch up.

"I see you are getting better at using your arm canes," Nicola smiled, patting his shoulder.

Jimmy was using three-inch-wide wooden boards with a crosspiece that fit under his arms, nailed to the top of the boards. Bands of thick leather helped to hold the pieces together. Mara cushioned the cross member to make it more comfortable when Jimmy's underarms leaned on them. He moved the boards forward and thrust himself to where the boards stood. It took him a while to get where he wanted to go, but it was much easier than carrying Jimmy around.

"How much longer must I use them? Ain't berry steady on my feet."

"I would say two weeks. If you don't, your leg will not heal properly, and you might have a permanent limp. I promise to check before I leave. Emmy can and will take care of it after I'm gone. Right, Em."

"I would be pleased to do so. After all, Jimmy is one of my special workers."

As he struggled to sit in a chair. Jimmy announced, "If I must, I must."

The evening flew by. Everyone still seemed

exhausted from the encounter with the thieves. Emmy promised to take her entire family to the medieval village tomorrow to show them the buildings.

They all rode to the village site after breakfast. The children, along with Nicola and Mara, rode in the cart and had a great time with Petes and Jerkens. They had cleaned out the Stone Cottage to the wooden floor earlier in the week, so their visit was brief. Some items at the Farmhouse demanded our attention. However, Emmy failed to understand the scarcity of artifacts. No matter how hard she tried, Potts' interest in the buildings perplexed her. Emmy had no intention of giving up the search.

They had just returned to the manor house when they heard a carriage drive up. "I bet it's Mother and Father," Nicola cried out as she ran to them. After all the hugs, they entered the sitting room and met Greyson.

"I understand you'll soon be a member of our wonderful family? Welcome," said Catherine. She reached out and gathered him in her arms. "You will soon learn we are different from most people in our class. We love to hug family members."

James, Emmy's foster-father, shook Greyson's hand. "Welcome, young man. Please take care of our youngest daughter and treat her with care, or I will make you very sorry." He patted Greyson on the back and then laughed.

After they sat down, minus the lads and small children, who were playing with the dogs on the front porch, the entire adult family organized a country wedding. After the excitement of the last few days, everyone looked forward to a pleasant and wonderful wedding day.

Mara agreed to make a special wedding dress for Emmy. Early the next morning, the three women went to the attic, hoping to find some usable material. It wasn't long before they found some antique white lace curtains packed in a trunk. Mara would design a dress to make Emmy look enchanting. Nicola and Emmy supervised the men, making the area presentable for a ceremony.

Emmy locked the trophy room door to keep anyone out. It would keep prying eyes and sticky fingers away from anything that they had found at the excavation site.

The sun broke through the clouds on Emmy and Grey's wedding day. The front porch, where the ceremony would take place, was overflowing with flowers of every shape and kind from the manor house's magnificent garden and greenhouse. Taking a deep breath when she opened the front door, Emmy could smell the roses.

Having an early breakfast with her sisters and their children on the day of the ceremony added the perfect touch. Emmy couldn't remember enjoying herself so much as laughter filled the room. The children were delighted with all the activity, and the girls danced in a circle when they heard they would be part of the actual wedding ceremony.

The little boys had many sword fights with miniature weapons Grey made for them. Emmy and Nicola fashioned flower and greenery crowns for the girls to wear at the wedding.

The lads and the men stayed at the manor house the night before the big day. His Grace insisted the newlyweds would have their reception in the manor house ballroom. He was very proud of the couple's work, and after all, Emmy was family-distant but still family.

Dressing in her room with her sister's help added to Emmy's enjoyment of the day. Reminiscences of childhood elicited mirth and tears, and then a knock interrupted them before the ceremony. Nicola went to answer it and found her mother and Brishen.

"Afternoon. Emmy is a beautiful bride." Nicola beamed.

"We would like to speak with the bride in private." Her mother smiled and kissed Nicola and Mara's cheeks.

"Mara and I need to check on our children, as it is almost time for them to get ready. We are once again off on a mission." The two sisters left arm in arm.

Brishen took one look at Emmy. "You, my dear, are a magnificent bride." Emmy stood like a statue. "I don't believe I've ever seen a more beautiful one. You look so much like your mother."

Emmy stopped in mid-stride and stared at Brishen. "You knew my mother?"

"Did you ever wonder, like your sisters, who your parents were?"

"Not really. They didn't want me, so I didn't care." Emmy walked over to Catherine.

"I had the best upbringing. This wonderful woman took care of me and loves me with her whole heart." Emmy hugged her. "I'm not sure I ever thanked you for all you did for me, Catherine Highbridge. You and father didn't give me life, but you both gave me a wonderful family and your unceasing love."

"You shared your love with all of us and made our family complete, dear Emmy. Brishen needs to talk to you in private. Please never change, no matter what the world offers you." Catherine hugged and kissed her cheeks. "Be happy always."

With tears in her eyes, Emmy watched her wonderful foster mother walk out the door. She loved Catherine and felt honored to be her foster daughter. She would always be grateful to Catherine.

Brishen waited for the door to close behind Catherine and then reached out and took Emmy's hand. "I know you said you weren't interested in your birth parents. However, I have something important to share with you. I can no longer keep it to myself."

"Brishen, you have been an extraordinary person in my life. I can't explain why or how we formed a special attachment to each other. You taught me more than I realized. You should know you'll always have my love and friendship."

"Emmy, I am more than just a friend. I'm your father."

Emmy stared at him. "Say that again because I'm sure I misunderstood."

"No, my dear daughter, you didn't. I'm your father."

"I don't understand."

“I was in love with a wonderful young woman. We were so young. She wasn’t a Roma. She lived in another town. When she became pregnant. I honestly planned to marry her. Neither of our families was happy about the situation; in fact, they were distraught, which is an understatement.”

“You see, I was a Roma prince and would one day be the leader of my clan. I really couldn’t have an English wife. Her family took her away. I spent months trying to find her; my friends also made efforts to locate her. She had disappeared.” He closed his eyes and sighed.

Emmy reached out and took Brishen’s hand. “Father, I’m so sorry.”

“Her sister walked into our camp twelve months later and handed me you. She said your mother had died and gave me no other information. I’m so sorry.

“You were so cute—about five months old, all smiles and so happy. I was seventeen. I did not know what to do with a child, especially one who was part English. I went to see Catherine, as I knew she had taken in two little girls, only a little older than you. If she were to raise you. You could be content and happy, and I would see you. I would’ve had to leave the Roma camp if I had kept you with me. I had nowhere to go and no money. It doesn’t excuse my actions. I did what I thought was best for you.”

Emmy started to talk, and Brishen put up his hand. “Please let me finish…”

“Before we came to Rockhurst, I had a camp meeting and told them about you. Some had figured it out, at least to some degree. They voted you their princess. You are part of the Roma family and camp." He reached into his pocket, took out a small box, and handed it to Emmy.

"This is a necklace given to a Roma princess when she marries. It is hundreds of years old. I ask that you wear it on your wedding day today. Realizing that many will understand what it means, many people could and would shun you because you are a Roma princess."

Opening the box, Emmy found a beautiful necklace. Stones of every hue and size formed a semicircle around an enormous emerald, which sparkled in the light. The chain was gold. She handed it to her father.

"Please put it on me. My hands are shaking. I'll be proud to wear it, my dearest father."

"Don't you think you should talk this over with Greyson first?"

"No, he loves me, not who my parents are. If you want to go down, talk to him, and then return to me. I'll wait right here."

Brishen was back in minutes. "I found your husband to be. He said to tell you he loves you and can't wait for you to be his wife."

Once Brishen left, Catherine stuck her head in the door. "I must go find your foster father and tell him he doesn't get to walk you down the aisle."

"Do you think he'll mind?"

"No, I told him the story about you and Brishen when we married. He'll understand."

Catherine left the room and called back. "Mara will come and get you when it's time, my dear."

Holding hands, Brishen and Emmy stood, not saying a word. If anyone looked closely, their eyes were the same color, and their smiles identical. It seemed only a second passed, and Mara was at the door.

"Come, dear sister. It is time to get you married."

They followed Mara down the back stairs. Roma guitars played a beautiful song. They strolled around the house toward the minister. Emmy reached a decision. She quickly whispered in her father's ear. He smiled and agreed. Brishen motioned to Emmy's foster father, and both men walked her down the aisle. Brishen took Emmy's hand and gently placed it on Greyson's arm.

Chapter 21

The ceremony was perfect in every aspect. There wasn't an unhappy face in the crowd of well-wishers, and the newlyweds smiled as they responded to the day's joy. The children were on their best behavior, and the women showed their pleasure in witnessing the wedding by crying. Of course, the men couldn't understand their logic.

The cooks from the lodge and the manor house outdid each other. People ate until they could not eat another bite. Just as it was growing dark, a carriage drove up to the front of the house.

A man began screaming. "Greyson! Come outside this instant! Your father has something to discuss with you." Grey's brother stood next to the carriage.

Clay, Barnaby, Brishen, and a few of his men followed Grey outside. The two men were now standing beside an opulent carriage. Before Grey could utter a word, the older man started berating

Greyson.

"I've been looking for you for months. You are to come home at once. You…"

Greyson stepped forward. "STOP. I'm not going anywhere with you now or ever. I don't know how you found me, but I can only guess."

The younger man spoke up. "You'll do as our father says. I'm your older brother. You must come home. You have an engagement to announce."

"Brother, what you and Father require is my money. You both have tried to run my life for as long as I can remember. NO MORE!"

Walking up, Emmy took Greyson's hand. "I would like you to meet my wife, Mrs. Emmy Hadden. These two men, my dear, are a poor excuse for a father and a brother. I have told you all about them in great detail."

"You did my husband. I want to welcome both of you to join us at our wedding ball as our guests. However, any folly from either of you and my father will escort you both off this property."

"Listen to me, both of you. I'm his father. Greyson must do as I say. He must obey me."

"Father, your demanding anything from me is in the past. I'm sorry for their behavior, my dear wife. Thank you for being so understanding of my situation. I'm sure this isn't the end of their plan. My dear, let us get back to our celebration. Oh, Father, it's time for you and my brother to leave."

Brishen quietly moved over to his men. "Watch the house. I believe they might come back tonight. If so, hold them. And come and get me."

Soon, father and son stood alone at the front

entrance. The wedding guests who had come outside to witness the commotion turned their backs on the two men and went back inside.

The two men continued to holler their fool heads off as they tried to make a scene. No one came out, so they finally left.

Candles in every window of the manor house lit up the house. Its appearance took on the look of a fairyland, complete with music floating on the evening breeze, creating a stunning landscape.

Dawn was breaking when the last guest left. Emmy could hardly keep her eyes open. It had been the most exciting day of her life. She knew Grey would be gentle with her. She, in truth, couldn't wait to be alone with him.

The newlyweds believed the guests from out of town were staying at the manor house. They didn't pay enough attention to what was happening. Brishen left more than an hour ago. One minute he was there, and the next he wasn't. Clay and Barnaby escorted the couple to the hunting lodge. They locked all the doors and windows after Emmy and Grey went upstairs. The men met Mr. M. on the stairs. He had a pistol in his belt and assured them he knew how to shoot it.

"I'm planning to stand watch inside the back door. Joeson put Petes and Jerkens outback. They have been roaming this fine night. There's this little nook where I got a pillow and a blanket. I assure you both I will be most comfortable."

"Thank you, Mr. M., we appreciate your help. Brishen and his men are the sentries outside. Do you think the dogs will bother them?"

"No, sir, I made sure they met all of them. Once done, the dogs stand down. Unless someone gives them a command, if anyone else comes along whom they have not met, there will be no guarantee what will happen."

Brishen and his men kept themselves deep in the shadows. Forming a ring across the open landscape, they didn't take long to reach the carriage. The driver sat atop and appeared to be sound asleep.

They found the dandies trying to navigate the area. First, they didn't have on proper clothes—their shoes belonged in the city. Brishen's men almost laughed the second time Grey's father fell on his face. They heard the dogs growl. The men dashed toward them, screaming their lungs out. Two Romas put out their arms, and the men stopped. The dogs stood back, bearing their teeth. Brishen spoke to the dogs in a calming voice.

"Glad they recognized me." Brishen's heart slowed down when the dogs lay down.

Mr. M. materialized. "I thought I heard the dogs. Are you gentlemen all right?" he asked.

Grey's brother shouted out. "Those dogs were going to attack us."

"I wasn't talking to you, Mr. Hadden. I was talking to the Romas."

"Mr. M., will you take the dogs back to the house? I'm going to talk to these men."

"Be happy to do as you ask. I can leave the animals if you prefer, as they can be very persuasive."

"Not necessary, but thank you for offering."

Once the dogs and Mr. M. had left, Brishen helped the two men to their feet. "I'm going to say this only once. You leave Greyson and Emmy alone, or I'll have your heads mounted on a silver platter. This is not a threat. It is a promise. Do I make myself clear?"

"Yes. But, but you don't understand. I have the title but nothing else, thanks to my wife's father. We have little money. Greyson's grandfather left most of his fortune to him, cutting us out of the picture."

"You are lying. Greyson's grandfather and mine were fast friends. When the last duke died, the title died with him. You inherited the land and monies entailed from your dear wife, but that was all. If you and your heir persist, I'll ensure that all of London has the complete picture.

I'm not a person you'd want to have as an enemy. My name is Brishen Draper. Inquire about me among your friends and acquaintances."

Mr. Hadden took a deep breath. "We shall see about this situation. Greyson has not heard the last of me. I promise you."

"Then you have not heard the last of me and mine. Escort these people to their carriage and make sure they leave the estate."

Brishen and two of his men watched the carriage leave as four Romas escorted the Hadden men off the property.

Buck, Brishen's right-hand man, asked. "Do you think we have to worry about them returning?"

"Time will tell."

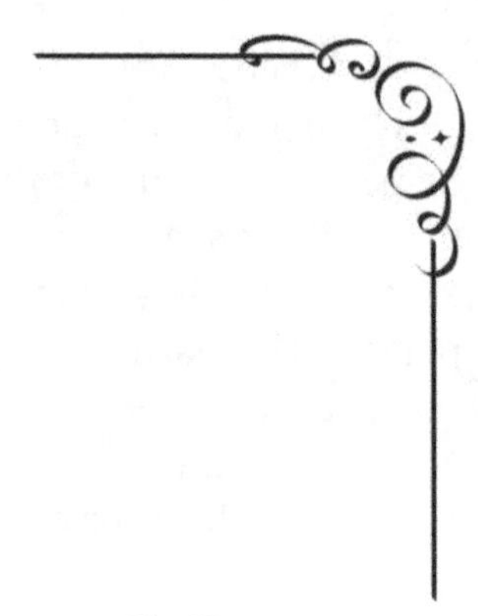

Chapter 22

The newlyweds didn't leave their love nest until early afternoon.

I seem to be smiling a great deal this morning. My wedding night was the most beautiful night of my life. It surpassed my expectations. Greyson was gentle and thoughtful. Always thinking about me before his own needs and wants. I wouldn't have stayed in bed with him the entire day, but there is tonight and all the nights of our lives. I can feel my cheeks growing warm; at least Grey and I are the only people in the room. No one else could know what I'm thinking.

The voices from downstairs filtered up to their room, and the newlyweds hurriedly got dressed and joined them.

"We figured if we all made enough noise, you both would join us. See how smart we are?" Barnaby grinned.

After a quick midday meal, Mara announced. "I

would like to go to Reed and see this little town. Eel's mother wants to close our dress shop in London and move to a smaller town. Reed may fit the bill. Especially now that Potts and his evil cohorts are out of the picture."

"I would be happy to escort you and anyone else who wants to come. Reed is only about a few miles from Rockhurst," Clay spoke up as he took Nicola's hand. "My father won't mind if we use his carriage. There is no way I could handle a trip, even for a mile, in the lad's cart. I'll secure the coach and driver if everyone wants to go."

The ladies agreed it would be a nice outing. Within an hour, they were on their way. One coach couldn't hold the entire group. Arriving in town in a few hours, they all strolled down Main Street. The stores were a delight, with the displays offering many local products. Shawls of every color imaginable and wooden toys for children. They purchased many items to take back home.

When Potts and his gang of thugs went to London, the authorities had either arrested the men Potts hired to protect his interests in Reed or they had disappeared.

Joeson's father and the townspeople welcomed the Rockhurst people with open arms once they all learned they had come to town. They organized an informal party as a gesture of thanks to everyone for their help.

They visited some smaller towns within a short distance over the next three days. On the fourth day, Nicola announced it was time to leave. She had much to do at home, as did Clay. Barnaby and Mara needed to inspect their farm, dress shop, and homeless shelter.

They spent the following day packing and couldn't believe how much more they had gained. Besides their many purchases, the townspeople gave them gifts for rescuing them from the clutches of Potts and his cutthroat gang. They discovered Potts had been bullying everyone in one way or another.

Jimmy was still up and about on his walking sticks. Nicola told him that after three more days, he could stop using them. Emmy announced that after her family left, they would go to the village to close up the buildings. The Stone Cottage floor required one more cleaning. They still had to replace the boards covering the windows. The Farmhouse still had a few artifacts to examine.

A few weeks ago, the lads discovered a small building that might contain some noteworthy artifacts. Time would tell.

Jimmy's bruises were gone unless you looked closely. You could see a slight discoloration of green mixed with yellow, and of course, purple. Jimmy's energy level returned, which was a problem because he had never learned to move at a leisurely pace until now.

Emmy's family packed the carriages and left for London the following day. Of course, packing all their bags and loading them onto the transport took longer than they expected.

Using one of Clay's father's wagons had been

necessary, as all their items and those they gained would not fit in one carriage. Corralling the children had been a real challenge. They didn't leave until late afternoon.

CHAPTER 23

The early morning found all the workers in the sitting room, having breakfast. They were tired from all the extra activities that had taken place during everyone's visit. But in truth, they were glad to be back at their work.

They first traveled to the Stone Cottage, wanting to ensure everything was in order and nothing had changed since their last visit. The next stop was the Farmhouse. Tucked in one corner was the final accumulation of material still to be examined. Emmy instructed the lads and Grey to secure the exteriors of both buildings and search for anything that needed attention.

Emmy entered the Farmhouse with Jimmy right behind her. On the floor was a rug, which sat almost in the center of the room. Emmy resolved to salvage it. It would just need a proper cleaning, which would happen much later. She rolled it up and then dragged it over to the side of the wall. Emmy went to the corner and began examining what remained, and she found a small wooden box near the bottom of the pile. Taking it to the doorway, which offered better light, Emmy opened it. Inside was a large key that slanted to one side, allowing it to fit inside the box. A note in English startled her.

This key will offer riches beyond your wildest imagination.

She chuckled because the building lacked any containers. Clearly, whoever had written the note had a sense of humor, which didn't amuse her.

"Miss Emmy, can I be walking around inside this here building? Standing or sitting in one place makes me leg hurt. 'Effing, I keep moving me leg, it don't be bothering me so much."

"Let me help you." Emmy walked over to help Jimmy up in case he faltered, because the floor was uneven.

He staggered the width of the building until he got the rhythm of his arm canes under control. Emmy returned to her previous activities. Moving across the floor, Jimmy counted the floorboards out loud. Emmy monitored him; she didn't want him to reinjure his leg.

Throwing the last discarded material stacked in a corner into an old bucket, which had seen better days. Emmy realized she only had to sweep the floor. The few artifacts they had found did not make the venture successful.

Jimmy stayed out of Emmy's way. Changing direction when necessary, he walked the length of the room. Without warning, Jimmy hollered out. Emmy watched him, frozen in place, as he tipped first one way and then another. Somehow, he stayed upright for a few seconds. Yet Jimmy found he couldn't keep his balance. He slid to the floor with his injured leg out straight.

Emmy rushed over to see what had happened to him in the fall.

"Are you hurt?" she blurted out.

"I be fine. Look, this be why my walking stick got stuck in the floor. Might be why I fell."

"This floor is so dirty. I can't see anything but grime."

Emmy felt on the floor until she found a depression on one floorboard, but the dirt covered it and appeared packed down. Jimmy took a small knife from his pocket and dug up the soil from inside the indent in the floor. Finally, he blew as hard as he could on the spot, causing dust and dirt to fly everywhere. This wasn't a hole. It was a depression with a metal ring embedded in it.

"Miss Emmy, do you think this is a trapdoor? I seen one once."

"Let me call the others. We should all discover what you have found together."

Emmy ran to the door and called to everyone to come to the Farmhouse. It didn't take long for everyone to gather in the building. Emmy directed them to the wall on the left side of the door.

She moved away from Jimmy. "Show them what you found."

He had the biggest grin on his face when he hobbled to the ring on the floor. "I be needing some 'elp to open it."

"Open what?" Jeb scratched his head.

"The trapdoor, or at least that is what Emmy and I think it be."

Greyson and Joeson grabbed the ring once Jimmy showed them, using one of his arm canes. There was still a lot of dirt on the floor. If you didn't know where the ring was, you would miss it.

"Wait," said Eel. He ran outside and got a container of rainwater. Taking a broom, he swept around the lines near the ring on the floor. Upon closer inspection, he found visible cuts on the wooden floor. He took a glass bottle, filled it with water, and poured it over the area. "Want to see where the door be."

"Good thinking, Eel," Emmy touched his shoulder.

Grey and Joeson pulled on the ring, walking toward the back of the building. Once opened, the trapdoor rested on the wood floor. They all stood transfixed at the big opening in the floor. It was easy to see some steps leading downward. Emmy lay on the floor and stretched out her arm, holding a lantern, trying to see what was beyond the steps.

She finally stood up and said, "Joeson, please go fetch The Duke. He should be here for our discovery."

"Yes, Miss." Joeson ran out the door and, in record time, was riding away.

Everyone in the building walked in circles, eager to see what was in the cellar. The lads played a guessing game. The adults didn't speak; they just stood in place or kept walking in circles. Because of nervousness, they couldn't stand or sit still.

Finally, Emmy got everyone except Jimmy cleaning up the wood floors as best they could. Using brooms, they created a minor dust storm. She opened the outside door, hoping the fresh air would replace some of the dust.

Eel gathered wet rags and pushed them around with his feet to clean up some of the dust and dirt. It didn't take long for Jeb to join him. Of course, the lads made it a game. Before they knew it, the floor looked better and was almost clean. They were all waiting outside when they heard horses galloping toward the building.

"It didn't take you long," Grey said as he watched them dismount.

"I met the Duke halfway to the lodge. He was coming to see us."

His Grace walked over and shook Greyson's hand. "Joeson said you discovered something needing my attention. He wouldn't tell anything else. He refused even to give me a hint. I even threatened to fire him, and he still wouldn't tell anything." The Duke slapped Joeson on his back and laughed.

Sir, you must come into the Farmhouse." Emmy beamed.

They entered the building. Emmy went in first because she wanted to see the look on the Duke's face when he saw the opened trapdoor. Eel and Jeb helped Jimmy navigate the entrance. She and the three lads stood in front of the opening in the floor. Greyson and the Duke entered along with Joeson.

"Your Grace, we wanted to show you what

Jimmy discovered." The four of them moved to the side so the opening in the floor was visible.

"You found this today? Just now, before Joeson came to get me? What is down there? Are there any steps? Have any of you ventured down? Do you know?"

"No, we thought you deserved the privilege of being the first to see what awaits us. After all, this is your land, and you have allowed us to conduct an archaeological excavation."

Emmy was relieved and thrilled to realize they might have found what they had been looking for. She kept her excitement to herself as she couldn't get her arms around such a marvelous find. Perhaps this is what Potts has been seeking. Not the cellar, but what is in it.

"Please, Your Grace, we have all been waiting a long time. Can we go down there now?" said Eel.

"Young man, how about you lead the way? I'll follow up with Jimmy, and Jeb can come right after me."

Grey spoke up. "I can carry Jimmy down on my back with the help of Joeson. Emmy can follow me."

"Absolutely not," Emmy stated. "I'm in charge of this endeavor and won't go last. In fact, I'll go first."

"It could be dangerous. I don't want to see you hurt," stated Grey.

"I'll lead the way." Emmy walked forward and grabbed the lantern right out of Grey's hand. "Follow me."

Grey locked the door so that no one could come

and interrupt them. They knew they no longer had to worry about Potts, but someone else could be watching them.

Emmy started down the steps with Eel close behind her.

Eel shouted so that everyone could hear him. "The steps are stone. Me don't think they be dangerous."

Jeb disappeared down the steps. Greyson followed Jimmy, then his Grace, then Joeson. They all stood together and looked around them. No one said a word. They could see enormous trunks, pictures, and bundles of wrapped goods. Identifying them was impossible because a shield covered most of the items. They would have to take all the items upstairs to determine their contents.

"We should bring up one article at a time, at least the first few, to see what they are. I want to make a drawing of this cellar before we move anything in it. I told you that you must identify the location of every artifact before you move it."

Running up the stairs, Grey retrieved Emmy's bag, which contained all the logbooks and art supplies she used to draw pictures. Each person placed their lantern on a step. The area near the stairs were well-lit. Emmy had different individuals measure the locations of the various items. It appeared the entire floor was the same size as the room upstairs. The area was overflowing with stored items.

Emmy divided the large area into numbered sections and drew a picture of each. It took her about an hour before she felt there was enough information to start the seek-and-find, which was her favorite expression. Her heart was beating so fast. Could anyone else hear it? Emmy wanted to remove the articles at the location closest to the steps. It would maintain some order to the artifacts, making it easier to identify where they came from within the building. Someone had stored the items this way long ago for a reason. Emmy hoped she could figure it out.

She drew a picture of the cellar's condition. The construction had used local stone, and she didn't believe it would collapse. She noticed no earthy smell, indicating that neither dirt nor moisture had reached anything. This might account for the excellent condition of the items they had looked at.

Joeson and Greyson carefully lifted the first trunk out of its place and took it up the stairs. Everyone followed and stood back as His Grace approached the chest, opened it, and raised the lid. He moved out of Emmy's Way.

"I believe you should be the first to see what is inside."

Emmy took two steps, held up her lantern, and took a deep breath. She handed her lantern to Jimmy. "Time to see what you have found, young man." She reached in and removed the first bundle.

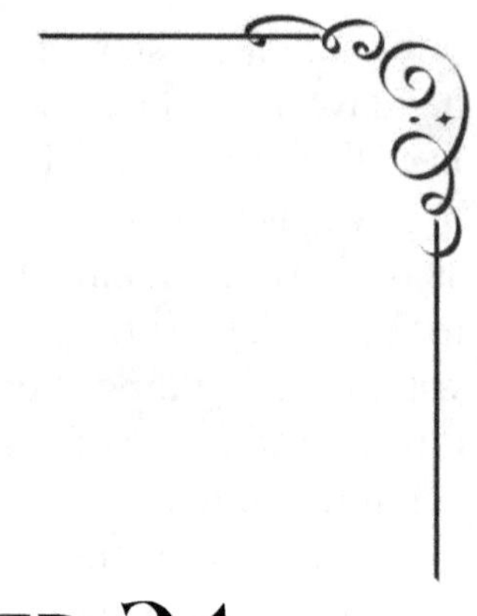

CHAPTER 24

By this time, Greyson had returned upstairs and brought up a small table. Its top side was very ornate, with hand-carvings of animals running along the edge. “I show you on the drawing where I appropriated it from.”

“Thank you. It’s much easier to look at what is inside at this level than to look at it on the floor.”

Emmy strained to untie the cording holding the bundle together, but found it impossible, as did Grey and Joeson. She took the knife Jeb offered and cut the cord, but only once. Preserving the rope with the packet was vital.

She and Grey unboxed the package with caution. Inside was a bound manuscript. The leather cover was in perfect condition. She studied it, determining whether to open it or wait until they reached the lodge. Emmy looked at all the faces and decided it was time to open it. There was no sound, and all eyes were on her. She tried to remain calm.

How long has it been since another human being looked at this book? It may have been hundreds of years?

Emmy opened the book and gasped, as it was a written record of the "Sumptuary Laws."

"I have heard of these laws but have never seen a copy. These English laws dictated how people could dress and act in society hundreds of years ago."

"Please read a few of the entries." His Grace beamed at Emmy.

Year 1281

"Related to food expenditure. King Edward III

Year-1336, 1337, and 1363

"King Edward III passed these to regulate the dress of various classes of the English people, promote English garments, and preserve class distinctions through costume, clothes, and apparel."

"Attempted to curb expenditures and preserve class distinction."

"No knight under the estate of a Lord, Esq., or gentleman, or any other person, shall wear any shoes or boots with spikes or points exceeding two inches, under the forfeiture of forty pence."

"Women were, in general, to be dressed according to the position of their fathers or husbands."

"Wives and daughters of servants could not wear veils worth over twelve pence."

"Handicraftsmen and yeomen's wives could not wear silk veils."

"Wearing fur by women could only be allowed if the knights received over twenty marks per year."

"Wives and daughters of a knight could not wear gold cloth or sable furs."

"The wife or daughter of an Esq. gentleman could wear satin, ermine, or velvet."

"The wife or daughter of a laborer would not wear clothes which cost more than a certain amount or have her girdle garnished with silver."

"Royal families were only allowed to wear gold and purple silk cloth."

"The Lombards and other foreigners could not import silk or lace. It was forbidden."

Year 1337

"Was designed to promote women's garments and restrict the wearing of furs."

"Distinguished several local categories and made members of each class easily distinguished by their clothing."

"This is just an example of what is in this book. However, laws of this type ended in the seventeenth century. It was to distinguish their class, and they had no choice."

"Who were the Lombards?" Jeb asked as he scratched his head.

"They were Germanic people who ruled most of the Italian peninsula centuries ago," Grey said as he moved next to Emmy.

Setting the book on top of the wrapping material, Emmy put it on the table. "This is most interesting and very informative, at least to me. I suggest we load up the cart and caravan and return as much as possible to the lodge. Many of the items are likely to be fragile and difficult to inspect here. I don't want them handled more than necessary. Otherwise, we'll be here for hours just inspecting, unwrapping, and re-wrapping artifacts."

"I agree with you." The Duke beamed at the discovery. "We must empty the entire cellar as soon as possible. We must take all items to the lodge for examination. I prefer not to have others assist you, as I want to keep this hush-hush for now. We'll discuss our next step once we have discovered what is in the trunks and bundles of clothes. Questions anyone?"

"No, Your Grace," Emmy stood off to one side. "Let us move as much as we can today. Jeb and I'll record what we removed from the cellar."

They placed the first containers and trunks of all sizes on the cart and caravan in no time at all. The trip back to the lodge was strange. Excitement was in the air, and yet no one made a sound. After last week's enjoyment, this was just too much. Emmy knew they had found the genuine treasure, more than she had ever dreamed of uncovering. Now, they would be in the thick of a new challenge. This proved to be a shock, yet something she had hoped for and prayed for.

When they returned to the lodge, they had their mid-day meal, still packed in four baskets. They dined on venison steaks, gravy, potatoes, and cabbage salad in the sitting room. The dogs guarded the wagons. Once finished, they cleaned up, unloaded the remaining artifacts, and hauled them upstairs to the storage area.

Eel approached Emmy. "We wonder, can we

return to get another load? It still be early."

"I had the same thought. Let's find Grey and Joeson. If they agree, we'll go."

They hurried back to the Farmhouse in the carts. This time, the trip was more jovial. They started back to the lodge just as it was growing dark.

The entire group gathered in the room before sunrise the next morning. Mr. M. had lanterns lit when Emmy entered. Everyone turned to look at her.

"My, we are all here so early this morning."

Eel moved toward her. "We be so excited. We could hardly get to sleep last night."

"I know. I heard the three of you moving around in the hallway and going back and forth between rooms.

"We didn't mean to keep you awake. Just couldn't be 'elping it. The open chest keeps calling us—at least in our minds." Jimmy grinned.

"I know you do not want to continue to imagine what is in any of the bundles or boxes. The three of you want to touch and feel everything. Before we can start examining them or removing anything, I'd like to show you all a drawing I've made of the cellar. I'm sure you didn't see Grey and me as we brought everything into the lodge. We marked everything before we left the Farmhouse. I have a drawing to show the position of each item in the cellar. We must continue to keep excellent records."

Greyson announced, "Emmy, Joeson, and I have set up some crude tables, old doors with some makeshift legs, which we'll use as we go through the items."

"All of us have assigned tables." Emmy beamed. "You'll receive some artifacts to determine what they are. I'll go around the room from time to time, logging in the book what you have. Then, place them back in the container or cover them with a cloth. You'll put them in the last room at the end of the hallway.

It's essential to keep everything as we found it. Are there any questions? Now is the time to ask," Emmy moved to stand next to Grey.

"You mean the three of us will be …'elping you with the treasures?" Eel beamed, as did Jimmy and Jeb.

Emmy said, "Yes, we trust you to do an excellent and thorough job. His Grace informed me he plans to schedule a meeting in London in three weeks. Our book must record all the artifacts. I don't see us doing so much in such a short time. However, we shall try our best."

Every person hurried and devoured their breakfast. It was a constant flurry of activity; Emmy and Grey helped the lads. Joeson removed coverings, including cording, ribbons, wrapping, or cumbersome material.

There was one chest Emmy wouldn't let anyone open. It was too heavy for her to move, so Grey and Joeson dragged it to her table.

"How did we ever get this upstairs yesterday?" Emmy shook her head.

Chapter 25

She thought the worktable could not stand the weight, so she had them leave it on the floor. It took her a long time to open it. Interruptions kept her busy, as she had to catalog each item someone found. There were gold plates, cups, and carved wooden pictures. Most of the items inside the container were free of dirt and grime.

"Miss, look what I found." Eel handed her two daggers, each with a cross emblem.

"Oh my, these are Templar daggers. The crosses are very distinctive."

"Who be the Tem…Templars?" Jeb asked as Jimmy and Eel joined him.

"During the Crusades, these Catholic knights protected Christian pilgrims and devoted their fortunes and lives to this cause for almost two hundred years.

"Their clothes were white with the Templar cross on the front. Anything you find with this emblem would have belonged to a Templar. These are in immaculate condition. Successful find."

Eel returned to his table with a Bible with the same symbol. Many items wrapped in white cloth seemed to have belonged to a Templar Knight.

"Miss, what happened to these knights? Ain't never heard about them before." Jeb touched the red cross on the dragger.

"The King of France desired their wealth and territory because they were rich. He destroyed the entire organization.

Jimmy appeared with three ampoules. "What be these, Miss Emmy?"

"Their usage was in sacred ceremonies and usually held holy water. They are called ampoules, roughly spherical flasks with two handles."

Jeb, not to be outdone, brought some metal and glass ornaments. "What be these?"

Emmy picked one up. "These are medallions. They encouraged pilgrims to purchase them and then place them as an offering to a saint to express devotion."

Jeb's genuine interest appeared to be in books with illuminations. He returned to Emmy's table with a manuscript of gleaming gold-leaf pages, ink, and paint. The language stopped him from reading the words on the pages, which enthralled him. Early calligraphers were often monks and priests who lived in monasteries. During the Middle Ages, religion had a profound influence on most art forms.

"I will ask His Grace if he has any books in the early English language for you to read."

"Oh, Miss Emmy, that be wonderful."

She finally told everyone to take a break to get some tea and sweets. The moment they were out the door, Emmy attacked her wooden chest, still sitting at the end of her table.

Chapter 26

It was a large container with leather straps around the entire trunk. Looking closely at the heavy metal fastener Emmy found in the center of the front, she noticed a large ring that she used to open the container's lid after releasing the buckles.

Opening it, she carefully touched the soft material wrapped around a chalice, which she was sure was solid gold. The large size meant they would use it only during a meaningful religious ceremony or a possible symbolic meeting.

Standing back, she marveled at the design of the crest. It might take some time to figure out what it meant. Her hand shook as she reached and pulled out an item wrapped in sheep's wool. The size made it cumbersome for her to move by herself. Placing it on the worktable, she carefully unwrapped a candlestick.

Further down, Emmy found four similar candlesticks; each was a different size. Emmy couldn't lift out the huge bundle at the bottom. It wasn't easy to see as there wasn't much light. She would get more lanterns when she heard the lads trudging up the stairs. Emmy quickly stood back as she wanted to watch their faces when they saw the candlesticks.

"Emmy…Oh, what have you found?"

Jimmy and Jeb trailed behind their leader. All three stood there, their faces filled with wonder. "Can we touch them?"

"I don't see why not." Emmy motioned for them to stand next to her so all could see the look on the men's faces when they entered the room.

"Here's your tea, milady." Grey had a tray with cups, a teapot, and fresh scones. He bowed until he saw the candlesticks. "These are beautiful." He pointed to the table.

"Oh, wait, I imagine it will get better." She motioned to the trunk. "There is something unbelievable at the bottom, but I couldn't lift it out."

Grey and Joeson pulled it out and set it on the counter.

Emmy frowned. "I still don't understand where all these artifacts are coming from. This set should be in a church somewhere. Don't you agree?"

"Do you remember what Joeson's parents told us about the old village story? A long time ago, someone's relative was part of the group gathering artifacts from the Catholic churches before King Henry VIII's knights could confiscate everything during the dissolution."

"I remember. We knew Potts was looking for

treasure, but I didn't believe a word of the old story. I know we have discovered the riches of the century. Can you imagine what could be in those other trunks and bundles we brought into the lodge? It'll take us years to figure this out. Joeson must get…"

Everyone looked at Joeson as he said, "I know His Grace."

They all sat around the table again, waiting for their benefactor to arrive. Emmy couldn't wait to see the look on his face. This time, she didn't have to wait long. She could hear Joeson. No, it seemed His Grace was speaking, and didn't seem happy.

"Good morning, once again. Joeson wouldn't tell me why I had to come. I suppose I could dismiss him, but who would care for my dogs?" He smiled.

The lads, Grey and Emmy, moved away from the front of the table so his Grace could see the altar artifacts.

He stood transfixed, slowly strolled over, and stood before the table. He reached out his arm to touch the gleaming cross. "May I?"

Emmy smiled from ear to ear and said, "Yes, Your Grace. After these long years of being under lock and key, I don't believe you can harm solid gold. We have uncovered beautiful objects. Let us show you a few other priceless items."

Chapter 27

Emmy took his Grace over to the table where Eel had been working. Beaming with pride, Eel showed him jewelry, medieval silver, and pewter bracelets, brooches, and cloak pins. Some featured engravings, while others featured semi-precious stones.

"Once properly cleaned, they will look as good as they did hundreds of years ago." Emmy rested her hand on Eel's shoulder.

Jimmy's table featured rings with large stones and elaborate engravings. Medieval hair accessories sat in the center of the table.

Jeb had stacks of manuscripts, books, and scrolls on his table. Anyone who found any written works made a point of bringing them to him. Jeb quickly became the keeper of these objects as he tried to understand them. He found some old books about language in the small library next to the trophy room. While

Eel and Jimmy played games, Jeb studied.

Grey and Joeson's table had a mismatch of many things. Knives and swords were under the table, and massive trunks hid a portion of a suit of armor. Their list included items they found: a visor, a breastplate, armored elbow guards (courier), and chain mail.

Emmy stated, "I believe a full suit of armor exists. Once we find all the pieces, we shall put them together." She was optimistic that there would be another container or two of armor—they just hadn't located them.

His Grace shook his head after he looked at all the unpacked items. "I never envisioned there would be such a discovery at Rockhurst. Let us go downstairs for tea. We'll have a natter regarding your discovery. I plan for all of you to attend an extraordinary meeting in London.

After blowing out the lanterns and securing items that could easily fall or break, they followed His Grace to the sitting room. They had opened fewer than ten containers of artifacts at this point. Emmy found she would become overwhelmed if she pondered what lay ahead.

Sitting at the table, His Grace announced. "We will travel to London in three weeks. My plans do not include telling the attendees where this discovery took place. Emmy will showcase a few items, and each of you will bring your favorite for everyone to see.

"This announcement will have a significant

impact on the archaeology community, the Catholic Church, and the English government. I wish Miss Emmy to receive the credit she deserves."

Excitement filled the room; the lads had wide grins on their faces. How they stayed sitting in one place was beyond Emmy; she could hear their trademark giggles. She would miss that sound someday. Right now, it was music to her ears.

The afternoon ended with champagne to celebrate a most successful archaeology excavation. The first two weeks flew by. They gathered in the storage area and continued cataloging the leather bags, containers, and trunks every morning. They made numerous trips to the Farmhouse to collect more artifacts. The group touched every item at least once.

Hard work never got boring because there was always a genuine surprise in store. No two items were ever alike. There was still something new to astound them.

Three days before they traveled to London, Grey brought Emmy a small, decorated miniature chest. "This might be the old box we have been looking for. I bet the key will fit in the lock."

"Do you have the key, dear husband?"

"Yes, I do." Grey grinned at his wife.

He placed the key in the lock. Emmy, shaking, turned the key, causing the top to pop open. By that time, everyone had gathered around her. They just stood and stared into the opening. Inside lay a flat, folded piece of what appeared to be parchment paper.

"Miss Emmy, ain't you going to open it?" Jeb moved closer to her.

With a sigh, she looked at him. "Of course, I was thinking about what someone might have written." Emmy picked up the paper and sat in her chair. Taking a deep breath, she cleared her throat as she opened the single sheet as soon as he felt the pressure of Grey's hand on her shoulder. She smiled as a tingle ran down her entire arm.

He gently squeezed her shoulder. "Perhaps this will give us the information we need." She smiled at him and opened the folded paper.

If you are finding this, I, Jerald Gilbreath, am dead.

I be needing to explain the treasure you done found. My friends and I didn't steal a bit of these goods. Various townspeople worked at many monasteries, cathedrals, hostels, and nunneries, and offered the items to us to protect them from King Henry VIII's greed. We not choose any of the goods. Them didn't care what we done with what they gave us. Just wanted it hidden from the King's guards when they came to take anything of value. Bilby and me be in charge, and our gang of Badder Boys helped us.

We be responsible for hiding the items until we decide what to do with the bounty. Six of us: Pike Villains: Bilby Seth, Janes Batgery, Phillips Bates, Simon Cuum and I. Our plan be to wait two years and then sell all them goods. Figure by then, someone would pay good money for the treasure.

Because of the war, most of the gang be dead. I be the last. I plan to return after participating in the Siege of Boulogne. It will be me last battle. If I'm not here to take the goods, they go to the finder, whoever you be. I had this written for me cause I can not read or write.

Simon X
Written for Simon Gilbert – 1544

Emmy touched Grey's hand. "Well, at least we now know how and why all these artifacts came to Rockhurst."

Joeson stood, "I know. I need to fetch His Grace. May I tell why we are requesting him here?"

"Yes, please do," Emmy said, with laughter in her voice.

In no time, the Duke came back with Joeson. "At least I know why I'm here." His Grace not only smiled but grinned.

Listening intently, he frowned after Emmy read the letter to him. "Mrs. Hadden, please find a safe place for this letter, as it will be our proof of ownership. It is time we gather the artifacts and proceed to London. We leave in three days, at dawn.

"I have hired Joeson's father, uncle, and two other men from the village to escort us. We'll take two carriages. Grey and Joeson will ride in one with the lads. Miss Emmy and I will ride with the artifacts to the Archaeology Society of London. We'll stay at my son's Woodhaven Estate until we go to the society's building.

The men and the lads will guard the artifacts. Emmy will arrive in a carriage within fifteen minutes of the meeting's start. Clay and Barnaby will escort her. Are there any questions?"

Emmy frowned. "Your Grace, do you think we'll have any trouble?"

"No, I don't foresee any problems before the meeting. After seeing the artifacts, I expect a general fuss and the usual questions. We'll leave early the next morning at first light, following the announcement, and be long gone before anyone can pay us an uninvited visit. If they can't find us, they won't be able to ask us questions we don't want to answer. No one must know where we have been. Grey, and I would expect your father and brother to appear."

"I'm afraid they will cause problems."

"My dearest Grey, they are not your responsibility. I'm sure we'll be able to handle them." His Grace reached out and touched his shoulder.

They all traveled through the storage area, which had taken over most of the upstairs rooms, including the attic and the vacant servants' rooms. They moved the maid's rooms to the manor house. Some artifacts found a place in every bedroom, in any available corner. Every person selected their favorite items to take to London.

Getting their attention was easy. Emmy clapped her hands. "Remove your items, which will go into the main storage area in London. From there, they'll go to the carriages. Remember, you are responsible for your items. Grey and I will supervise the preparation."

It took the better part of two days to prepare everything. They decided one coach couldn't handle the weight. To split the load and leave more room in the carriages, they took a wagon. They loaded everything the night before their trip.

James and Keller guarded the coaches overnight and would stay to watch over the lodge, along with a few honest men from Reed.

The trip to London was uneventful, which was a blessing. They arrived late in the evening. They proceeded to the stable on the Woodhaven Estate. Wills, the head groom, greeted them.

The cargo found a place on a flatbed cart pulled by yet another ornery donkey, who didn't seem to appreciate having a harness around him so late in the evening. He tried to bite anyone walking near him. Finally, Eel punched the animal on the nose, which, to everyone's surprise, made it behave. Emmy fed the animal apples once they reached the kitchen.

Mr. Hirsch, the butler, was on guard duty in the library, watching over the artifacts. East End gang members stood outside to guard the treasure and the people. There was no discussion. Everyone was bone tired from the long trip.

Excitement and caution kept us awake during the trip.

The housekeeper escorted the guests to their rooms, and the house fell silent until sunrise. Then, it became a beehive of activity.

The breakfast fare found places on the sideboard. Everyone had something to choose from: a mixture of ham, eggs, bread, muffins, tea, and coffee. A bell pull was in the room in case a particular item needed to be requested. It only had to be pulled once, and a maid would appear to fill the request.

The staff took the cart to the stable to put the artifacts in the carriage for the trip to the museum. Clay, Joeson, Barnaby, His Grace, the lads, and the guards all climbed aboard a cargo wagon, which took them straight to the back of the Archaeology Society building.

The caretaker let them in. Everyone helped carry the artifacts into a locked room. The lads opted to stay in the room until it was time to take everything to the assembly for display.

People occasionally rattled the doorknob and tried to open the locked door. The lads continued to hear snippets about the meeting and questioned why someone had locked the room, as it was most unusual.

A brief return to London delighted the boys. Eel got to visit with his mother. Jimmy and Jeb were also happy to see Susanna Summers. They had moved in with Eel and his mother years before, when the London streets became unsafe for them.

Eel was pleased to call his mates his brothers; they felt the same way. Susanna adopted the boys, and they immediately called her mother. Neither Jeb nor Jimmy could remember their families, no matter how hard they tried. They had been very young when they had to fend for themselves on London's East Side.

Jimmy had a deck of cards, and the boys played Commerce, their favorite game. Of course, the boys tried to make up some of their own rules, which added to their fun.

Chapter 28

Emmy traveled to the Archaeology Society in a carriage, with two Bow Street Runners acting as her bodyguards. Her brothers-in-law arrived at the assembly early because they expected the Hadden men to attend. Most likely to cause problems.

The closer Emmy got to the building, the more nervous she became.

I don't know what type of reception I'll receive. However, I won't let that stop me—it's time to stand up for myself.

When the vehicle stopped, one runner opened the door. He assisted her down from the coach and walked her to the building's steps.

"Miss, I'll be waiting here until you be in the building."

"That is unnecessary."

"Yes, however, those were me orders." He touched his hat and bowed his head.

Emmy stood for a few minutes, watching society

men mount the stairs and enter the building.

No one is paying attention to me. It's time for me to gather my courage and enter.

Emmy climbed the stairs, taking a deep breath with each step. She counted them, as it seemed to quiet her overactive mind as she moved closer to the massive front door. Taking a deep breath, she put a hand on the door latch and pulled with all her might. The door gave just a few inches. Emmy crunched up her face and tugged the latch once again.

She finally opened it just enough to squeeze through the opening and enter the smoke-filled lobby.

A man standing near a small, tall table raised his hand to stop her. "Excuse me, Miss. Women may not enter. You must leave." He pointed to the door behind them.

Emmy straightened her back and looked directly at the man. "I have an invitation to the assembly." She removed it from her pocket and handed it to the man.

"I must get approval before I can allow you in." He turned his back and hurried out. Within a few seconds, three men returned with the original man, who still had Emmy's invitation in his hand. The older gentleman of the three cleared his throat and stated in a toplofty voice.

"Miss, this is highly irregular. This organization makes significant discoveries about England's past, which mere women can't possibly understand. Why you received an invitation is beyond my comprehension. There must have been a mistake.

I'm afraid you'll have to leave."

"I'm not leaving and plan to sit in the assembly." She grabbed her invitation from the guard and slipped past the men in the foyer. She heard them sputtering behind her, but kept moving toward the center of the lobby.

Emmy smiled because she knew they were in for a huge surprise. She walked around a group of men who stared at her.

"What in the world is a woman doing here? Someone should make her leave."

Some men chortled and said, "Maybe she is going to the back room."

Some blew smoke in her face. Emmy took a handkerchief out of her pocket, which she had earlier poured lavender oil into, helping dissipate the smoke odor to some degree.

The room appeared full when she spied a chair toward the back of the hall. She looked for Grey. As most men were much taller than she was, Emmy couldn't see past them. She felt the pressure on her elbow and looked to her right. Barnaby stood beside her. He whispered in her ear.

"As we figured, Grey's father and brother have shown up. Your husband and father are taking care of them. Not to worry, I wouldn't want Brishen to be angry at me or mine for a minute. Our seats are over here. Graham is holding them for us."

Many of the men in attendance appeared to remember Barnaby and his best friend Graham's membership in a notorious East Side gang during their youth. Most took a wide berth around them.

The chairman called the meeting to order. "I'm

very pleased to see the turnout for this special meeting sponsored by Duke St. George. He has exciting news regarding the recent discovery of medieval artifacts, among other findings. Today is a red-letter day for our organization. It is my pleasure to introduce Duke St. George."

Applause thundered throughout the hall. Excitement filled the air, and a murmur of voices speculated about the meeting's purpose. Emmy secretly smiled to herself.

His Grace walked up to the podium and stretched out the palms of his hands to quiet the room. "It's my pleasure to tell you about a recent archaeology excavation I've had the pleasure of being a small part of. I hired the right person to lead this endeavor, and to say I'm honored and proud of the work accomplished would be an understatement.

I've invited the archaeologist responsible for recovering priceless items from medieval times.

The members applauded and stomped their feet in enthusiasm. Once again, His Grace raised his hands to quiet the men down. "It's my pleasure to introduce Mrs. Emmy Highbridge-Hadden."

The room became silent as Emmy, Barnaby, and Graham moved to the front of the assembly and mounted the stairs. Once, Emmy was standing next to His Grace. One man in the center of the room stood.

"I have no plans to sit here and listen to a woman talk about excavations. She probably doesn't know what our society is about. I'm leaving, and ask those in agreement with me to stand up."

Half of the room stood and moved to the aisles to

leave. Emmy took a deep breath, moved forward, and exclaimed. “You can choose to leave and miss out on the chance to see the artifacts hidden from King Henry VIII’s knights after the dissolution of the Catholic churches in England.”

When Emmy felt all eyes on her, she trembled as she took the solid gold chalice from a cloth bag His Grace handed her when she came onstage. The artifact sparkled in the candlelight. The room was silent.

“This is solid gold, and one I believe is from a cathedral. I’ll continue when those who wish to do so have left or returned to their seats.”

No one left or said another word, not even the man who had made such a fuss. Everyone in the room was captivated. The men standing returned to their seats.

Eel was the first to bring out a medieval helmet with chain armor. He held the article high above his head and stood next to Emmy as she pointed out the item’s unique elements. “The top of the forged metal helmet features wide eye cutouts for optimal vision on the battlefield. The metal continues down across the nose to the chin. They attached chain armor to the back half of the helmet, which would protect the back of the wearer’s head.”

Next, Jeb brought out an illuminated manuscript. He opened the book to several pages, allowing the audience to see the blue lapis border and the gold adorning the pages as he walked back and forth across the stage. Beautiful calligraphy graced the parchment pages. He set it on a display table with a stand to keep it open. He left and returned with a gold, medieval-gilded manuscript cover. Emmy stated it originated in the eleventh century.

With Clay's help, Jimmy brought out his favorite item, a sword. It was gold inlaid with engraved symbols, including the classic Templar cross. Semi-precious stones decorated the hilt. The society's members in the audience stomped their feet and hooted.

Emmy discussed various found items, including rings, bracelets, and earrings. She explained how their historical value and ownership were determined.

The lads pushed a table on small wheels to the center of the stage. Barnaby and Clay held onto a cloth that covered the items on top of them.

Gesturing with her hands toward the table, Emmy said. "These items were part of a church's main altar and would have stood behind the chalice I previously displayed. If you gentlemen would remove the cloth."

The men moved to the front of the table and stood at each corner. Each man took a corner of the fabric and pulled it backward. The assembly gasped at the sight of the six marching gold candlesticks and the main altarpiece, which displayed a silver Jesus on a gold cross. The candlelight in the room highlighted the display's beauty. Men stomped their feet. The sound rolled back and forth across the room.

Once the room quieted down, Emmy said, "I know many of you have questions."

Someone shouted. "I would like to get a closer look so I can examine the items!"

The men covered the table and moved it from the stage. Emmy moved again to the center of the stage.

"Gentlemen, all in due time. Duke St. George has requested that the London Museum display these items. The museum will be adding additional items to the collection from time to time."

The guards returned the artifacts to the carriage and escorted them back to the Woodhaven Estate. Emmy and His Grace took center stage. The buzz of conversation ran throughout the room. Emmy put up her hands to quiet the room.

Questions continued to roll across the hall. The lads came out, signaling that the items were on their way. Emmy and His Grace left the stage.

Grey and Brishen marched up to them. Emmy could tell Grey was furious, but decided this was not the place nor the time to discuss his family's antics. She reached for his hand and gripped it, making Grey smile through clenched teeth. She hugged her father and kissed his cheek.

"Poppa, it's always nice to see you." She smiled. "We can talk at the house about your day?" She laughed at the look on Grey's face and her father's face.

"By the by, my brother announced his engagement to the young woman next door to them. She is an heiress."

Emmy, Grey, and the lads left for their return trio to Rockhurst the following day. Eel's mother came with them to make inquiries about opening a dress shop in Reed or one of the neighboring towns. Mara would be at Creations, the dress shop in London, which is now jointly owned by Susanna Summers,

Eel's mother, and Mara, Emmy's sister.

Emmy introduced Susanna Summers to Mr. and Mrs. M. They all strolled into the sitting room on their return. By the time they had removed their outer clothing, tea was waiting for them in the sitting room.

The trip back to Rockhurst had been uneventful. It took them four days, as they were in no hurry. His Grace stayed in London to work with the museum on the displays for the artifacts. He knew with no doubt that the British Government and the Catholic Church would try to lay claim to many of the discovered items. He, of course, had plans to stop them.

The dogs greeted them as soon as they drove through the gate. Joeson had left London on horseback and returned two days before them. He had been out hunting, and the dogs were always with him. They stopped to talk for a few minutes. The lads got out, and the dogs confronted them with big licks on their faces and hands.

They announced it was good to be home. Emmy looked at their smiling faces.

I agree; this is home. Soon, Grey and I'll have to think about leaving. My life has undergone significant changes since I arrived here. I hate to think of going anywhere.

She looked at the land and the lodge as they drove closer.

Mr. and Mrs. M. greeted them. "Tea will be in the sitting room in a few moments."

"How did they know we would be here?" Eel asked.

"Not sure. I think it's what we would call instincts."

Mr. M. laughed. "Welcome home."

They were back at work the following day, which never became monotonous. There were always discoveries that generated even more excitement. A beautiful medieval carved ivory relief panel depicting the Ascension, framed in a wooden three-panel screen. The centerpiece was higher than the end pieces. The details were outstanding.

"Emmy found another antique oak panel, dating from 1500 to 1550, carved with animals and people wrapped in animal hides. An iron crossbow bolt from the 14th to 15th century, and an iron spring scissors with a maker's mark, again from the 15th century. An iron rowel set of spurs, used in the 15th and 16th centuries, sat on the trunk's bottom, wrapped in wool."

Every day was a pleasant surprise. Eel and Jimmy cleaned up the chests, wooden boxes, and any containers they found among the artifacts. Eel and Jimmy handled the dirty work, cleaning and polishing each item. Some look almost new, while others have hand-carved inlays of gold and silver.

The list of objects continued to grow. Some, unfortunately, would never see the light of day because of their condition. Emmy refused to throw them away. Maybe in time, she or someone else would devise a way to preserve them.

One day, as they were quietly working. His Grace came into the room. Emmy looked up from her work as he stood silently watching.

"Welcome. We did not know you were coming

today. I hope you have gotten my letters outlining our recent discoveries." Everyone in the room came over to greet him.

His Grace said, "I must offer a toast to Emmy for her outstanding job of dealing with the society. You were marvelous."

Emmy sighed, "I appreciate everything everyone did to make this possible. I know we are far from over with our discovery, but thank you for believing in me, Your Grace."

Everyone applauded. "Grey and his father-in-law will tell us what happened with the Hadden men."

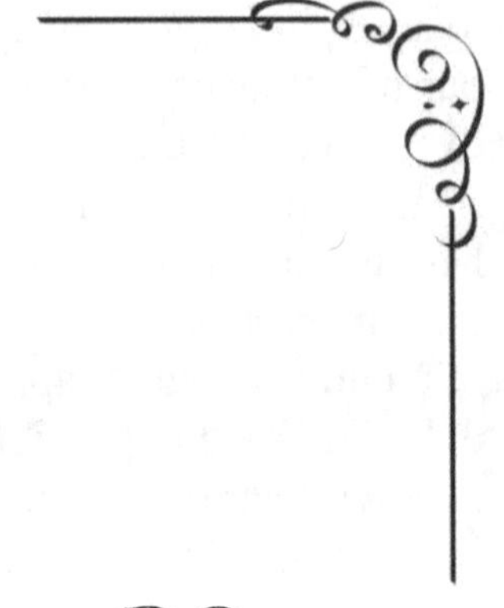

CHAPTER 29

"Dear Emmy, I'm very…I want to apologize for not being able to hear your presentation. My father and brother arrived just as you entered the assembly room, having spoken with many of the men in the front lobby. Brishen and I took them into one of the small meeting rooms."

"We decided it was best if they didn't hear about the artifacts. Of course, they are still seeking funding, which is nothing new. If I gave them funds, it would only last for a short time, and they would be back for more." Grey looked at Brishen.

"I have investigated and discovered everything they own or borrowed. Grey and I have paid up most of the delinquent debts."

Barnaby, Mara's husband, stood to refresh his drink. "I don't mean to sound harsh, Grey and Brishen. However, you know they'll return soon, looking for more and more money. Because they are gamblers at heart, it is hard for them to change at this stage. It is a tough habit to break. I have watched many men fall into this trap."

Grey stood and strolled over to Emmy. "I know; I've watched them all my life. Once my dear mother died, their problems only grew. We established small funds for them. It'll give each of them a small income. If they spend it foolishly, then it will be gone. We explained in great detail. I've no plans to change our plans now or in the future."

"We have mentioned their situation to a few key people. Time will tell, but we are determined to bring this handout to a close. They seem to think Greyson owes them."

"Early this morning, I asked Mrs. M. to prepare a special luncheon, as I have news for all of you. Where is Miss Susanna? I would like her to attend as well."

"She is in the workroom one downstairs," Emmy said.

"I thought that all the workspaces were on the upper floor."

"Your Grace, we renamed the trophy room to storage room one. Figured all the animal heads and rugs were …."

"Wonderful idea. Let's gather there. Shall we?" He took Emmy's arm and led the way. They formed a line going down the stairs.

Sitting at the table, Susanna was reviewing plans for the new dress shop she and her silent partner, Mara, hoped to open in Reed. She located a couple of storefronts and sat studying her options. When the door opened, she gathered her papers to leave.

His Grace stood back as everyone entered the

room and took a place at the table. “Miss Susanna, please don’t leave. I’ve called a meeting, and you are part of it.”

“Your Grace?”

“Yes, you, Miss. We shall wait for the food before I tell you why I have gathered us together.”

He had no sooner finished talking when Mr. and Mrs. M. came with an extensive buffet luncheon. The couple was getting ready to leave when His Grace announced he wanted them to stay and asked Mr. M. to please ask the cook and maid to join them. They gathered their food on their plates and seated themselves once again. Once everyone was in the room and sitting at the table, His Grace stood.

“I’ve asked you to sit here eating so I can discuss some plans the dear Duchess and I have made. I’ve enjoyed watching the excavation unfold over the last few months. You have all given me a new purpose in life. It’s been exciting to watch you learn to take part in this excellent enterprise. I’m so proud of this endeavor.

You lads have taken on a project way beyond your years and have been an integral part of the process. In doing so, you three have become young men.

I have found it most exciting to watch Emmy become the archaeologist I knew she could be. Grey, it has done my heart good to see you become the man you are. You and Emmy falling in love is one of the best outcomes of this endeavor.

“Joeson, thank you for all the hard work and the knowledge you have gained in raising and training my dogs. They love you. You have worked enormously hard on this project as well.

"The Duchess and I have tried to think of a way to thank each of you."

Emmy rushed, interrupting. "Before you say any more, Your Grace. Thank you for giving me this chance to become a known archaeologist. You trusted me and backed up my convictions with many individuals, including Mr. Potts. You never wavered in supporting me, the lads, Grey, or Joeson. I thank you more than you will ever know."

"Thank you as well." Grey reached for Emmy's hand. "Without you, well, just let me say-thank you."

"Our recognition of each of you is as follows. Grey and Emmy, the Duchess, Clay, Nicola, and I arc giving you fifty acres, including the Hunting Lodge and village, as a wedding gift. We hope this can be your primary residence for your archaeology projects."

His Grace held up his hands to keep anyone from talking. "Lads, all three of you will soon sit down with me to discuss what you want your adult lives to be. We'll support you in whatever you choose. Miss Susanna, we discovered your desire to live in Reed and own a dress shop. The Duchess and I'll be your silent partners with Mara."

"Oh, Your Grace. I can't…"

"Nonsense. You raised two boys with your son, giving them a safe home when they had none. You made them part of your family. This offer allows you to receive something in return, just for you."

Susanna pushed herself back in her chair as tears gathered in her eyes. "Thank you."

"Joeson, I'm hoping you will accept the Rockhurst manager position and a partnership in the ownership of the Rockhurst dogs. The Duchess and I have decided not to reside permanently at Rockhurst. We find it just too far from London. We will only visit occasionally."

"Mr. and Mrs. M. and the lodge's excellent cook, Molly, and Ivy, our young maid, we would like you to stay at the lodge and continue to provide for the Hadden family. Your salaries will increase if you wish to stay. We'll discuss your decisions at a later time. It is time I left, as you know, the Duchess is waiting for me, and I don't want to be late."

His Grace came and hugged Emmy, kissing her cheek. "You are the daughter we never had; I'll return soon to discuss more details with you."

Epilogue

Emmy and Clay plan to identify, label, and catalog many artifacts over the next two years. Once they complete the task, they will house these artifacts in the Rockhurst Collection and showcase them in the Duke and Duchess St. George Museum in Reed.

Six months ago, the dedication ceremony for the building and a party celebrating the opening drew the entire town. People from all over the world have been coming to see the items. Emmy and Grey rotated many artifacts between the British Museum in London and Reed. After the museum opened, Emmy and Grey began traveling to other archaeological excavations. While enjoying themselves, they never stay long, as the Rockhurst Estate Hunting Lodge calls them home.

The young lads, now young men, have gone their separate ways. Eel is attending a private school with plans to attend Oxford to fulfill his dream of becoming a barrister. Jimmy went to sea and returns between voyages. His further plans include owning a fleet of cargo ships and partnering with Barnaby. Jeb had become a scholar, studying illumination manuscripts and learning other languages at the lodge.

Joeson has become a world leader in breeding English Mastiffs and enjoys serving as the manager of Rockhurst.

Susanna and her partners own two dress shops, one in Reed and one in a neighboring village. Button and Bowes are very successful, and Mara continues to design clothes. The dress shop in London closed, but customers find their way to Reed.

Emmy and Grey are starting a family. Their first child will be born in six months.

All is well at the Rockhurst Village Estate.

About the Author

Z. Minor (my maiden name) is my pen name. The reason is simple: no one would be able to say or spell my married name without instructions, which is Louise Z Pelzl.

I have enjoyed reading all my life. My mother always told the story of me as a teenager, reading a book, my head bobbing to the music as I listened, and somehow watching American Bandstand.

I remember one day saying to myself, “It’s time to write my stories.” It took me 20 years to accomplish my goal, and then the rest is history. I started the Sisters of the Coin series many years ago. It took me moving to Kansas to finish and publish my first book, *Sisterhood of the Coin,* followed by *Mara’s Legacy*. Both are available on Amazon. *Emmy’s Discovery* is the third book in the series.

I enjoy developing my characters, who become almost real people to me as I write about them. Yes, there are times they talk to me, especially if they don't like what I have them do or say, etc.

I hope you enjoy my story, 'Emmy's Discovery', as much as I enjoyed writing it. I look forward to hearing from you. www.zminor@sctelcom.net.

www.ingramcontent.com/pod-product-compliance
Lightning Source LLC
LaVergne TN
LVHW020713110826
845149LV00012B/2243

* 9 7 8 1 9 7 0 5 6 0 2 5 1 *